## "I Need ... Evening—" Alex Began.

"And you want me to play the role?"

Alex nodded, and inside his pocket, his fingers clenched. The last place he wanted to be was here, staring into her incredible dark eyes and asking for help, but he was facing a thirty-day time limit to fulfilling his dreams.

"I'm having dinner with a man whose company I'm trying to buy. He thinks I'm newly married. After that, it's over."

"You keep the touching down to a minimum and no kissing."

Alex had to admire her candor. It was rare that a woman faced up to him. He was relieved she saw this the same way he did. As a job, an assignment. Yet, a part of him, the barren spot deep in his chest refusing to remain hidden when she was around, wanted to be more to her. Because his attraction for her ran too deep for comfort.

Dear Reader,

Welcome in the millennium, and the 20th anniversary of Silhouette, with Silhouette Desire—where you're guaranteed powerful, passionate and provocative love stories that feature rugged heroes and spirited heroines who experience the full emotional intensity of falling in love!

We are happy to announce that the ever-fabulous Annette Broadrick will give us the first MAN OF THE MONTH of the 21st century, *Tall, Dark & Texan*. A highly successful Texas tycoon opens his heart and home to a young woman who's holding a secret. Lindsay McKenna makes a dazzling return to Desire with *The Untamed Hunter*, part of her highly successful MORGAN'S MERCENARIES: THE HUNTERS miniseries. Watch sparks fly when a hard-bitten mercenary is reunited with a spirited doctor—the one woman who got away.

*A Texan Comes Courting* features another of THE KEEPERS OF TEXAS from Lass Small's miniseries. A cowboy discovers the woman of his dreams—and a shocking revelation. Alexandra Sellers proves a virginal heroine can bring a Casanova to his knees in *Occupation: Casanova*. Desire's themed series THE BRIDAL BID debuts with Amy J. Fetzer's *Going…Going…Wed!* And in *Conveniently His*, Shirley Rogers presents best friends turned lovers in a marriage-of-convenience story.

Each and every month, Silhouette Desire offers you six exhilarating journeys into the seductive world of romance. So start off the new millennium right, by making a commitment to sensual love and treating yourself to all six!

Enjoy!

Joan Marlow Golan
Senior Editor, Silhouette Desire

Please address questions and book requests to:
Silhouette Reader Service
U.S.: 3010 Walden Ave., P.O. Box 1325, Buffalo, NY 14269
Canadian: P.O. Box 609, Fort Erie, Ont. L2A 5X3

# Going...Going...Wed!

## AMY J. FETZER

Silhouette®

Desire

Published by Silhouette Books

America's Publisher of Contemporary Romance

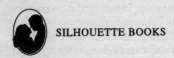

SILHOUETTE BOOKS

ISBN 0-373-76265-8

GOING...GOING...WED!

Copyright © 1999 by Amy J. Fetzer

This edition published by arrangement with Harlequin Books S.A.

Visit us at www.romance.net

**Printed in U.S.A.**

**Books by Amy J. Fetzer**

Silhouette Desire

*Anybody's Dad* #1089
*The Unlikely Bodyguard* #1132
*The Re-Enlisted Groom* #1181
*Going...Going...Wed!* #1265

## AMY J. FETZER

was born in New England and raised all over the world.
She uses her own experiences in creating the characters
and settings for her novels. Married nineteen years to a
United States Marine, and the mother of two sons, Amy
covets the moments when she can curl up with a cup of
cappuccino and a good book.

For Robert:

For loving me when I know it must be hard being my husband,

For suffering the teasing with a faint smile and a polite nod,

For believing I "still light up a room" after all these years, and being a little part of every hero I create.

You gave me the chance to pursue my dream,

And it was your faith in my ability that sent me forward.

We've come full circle, my love, and it's never ending.

*Semper Fi.*

# One

"**W**ell, I bet this is a first."

Madison Holt stood still as her friend Katherine arranged the beaded gown around her ankles. Tinkling crystal and murmurs of conversation filtered through the curtain hiding her from the guests assembled in the lavish, stone garden.

"What's that, sugah?"

"The oldest living virgin auctioned off to the highest bidder, and it isn't even my virtue that's up for sale."

Something close to a snicker sounded behind her, and Madison twisted as Katherine straightened and faced her, giving her that Davenport smile, the one that preceded her dignified Southern delivery that usually cut the strongest men off at the knees.

"White slavery is frowned upon in Savannah." Absently Katherine adjusted the thin, beaded strap on

Madison's bare shoulder. "But if you prefer, I can put your virtue on the block for the auction?"

"It is a thought." Might be the only way she'd lose it, Madison thought, before she reached twenty-five.

"Of course there would be a riot, I'm afraid."

Madison folded her arms over her middle and cocked her hip. "A rush of men? I don't think so."

Katherine pulled her arms apart with a warning look. "No. Women."

Madison's brows rose questioningly.

"I bet there isn't a single virgin out there." Katherine inclined her head to the velvet curtain. "And you know how they don't like being upstaged."

"Perish the thought," Madison said, her nervous stomach easing a bit.

But Katherine recognized her apprehension. "You can walk away right now, sugah. I won't force you to do something you don't want to do. Especially when it's my company that's donating an employee's time to this charity auction."

"No, I agreed. I'm here, in this gorgeous gown—"

"—which looks better on you than it ever did on me."

Madison glanced down at the borrowed plum-colored gown, hugging her figure like a second skin. It made her look like a mermaid. She was afraid to move in it or flop like a dead flounder on the stage. "I still don't see why I needed to dress like this."

"Packaging."

"Showing my breasts off like NASCAR trophies hardly speaks for my ability to whip up a balanced meal in twenty minutes."

Katherine blinked. "You can really do that, can't

you? In twenty minutes?'' Madison nodded cautiously, catching the admiration in her voice. ''*I* can't get out of the shower and dressed in less that thirty.''

Because Katherine never *had* to do it, Madison thought. But when the push was there, she thought, people did things they didn't normally consider. Like this. Allowing herself to be displayed for auction. Whoever bought the services of Wife Incorporated received a week of paid domestic service. It was Katherine who lost money by the donation. But then, God bless her generous heart, Katherine could afford to lose it.

Madison couldn't. It's why she'd agreed, even though she already had another part-time job. That and the double pay.

Madison gestured to the curtain. ''Tell them I'll swap a hog for a clean house. Nothing under a hundred pounds dressed out, though. I don't want to look cheap.''

Katherine rolled her eyes, smiling. ''Not a chance, honey. Dress or not.'' She nodded to the *X* on the floor. ''Take your place. It's show time.''

Madison's stomach clenched again, yet she stepped center stage behind the curtain leaning as Katherine bussed her cheek, then smiling when she rubbed away the lipstick smudge. Madison released a slow breath. Beyond the velvet curtain stood the cream of Savannah society. Anyone who lived north of Gaston Street, she thought with a smirk. They were dining on caviar canapés and sipping expensive champagne, waiting.

To make a bid on her.

She didn't think a clean house and home-cooked meals were going to make a difference to the affluent of Savannah. They'd likely bid and never use the certificate. Or maybe give it away. Madison didn't care. It was easy money as far as she was concerned.

"I know you don't like being displayed like this, sugah," she said in a loud whisper, and Madison glanced to her right. "And frankly it gets my garters in a twist, but the committee—"

"It's all right, Kat. And I'd simply die if your garters got twisted."

Katherine winked. "You're a peach, sister. Just pray Alexander Donahue doesn't get some wild notion to bid on you."

Madison's tapered brows shot up. Savannah's wealthiest most-eligible-and-meaning-to-stay-that-way bachelor needing a wife for hire? It was almost laughable. He had a notorious reputation of never staying with a woman for more than a date or two, and since Katherine's late husband and Alexander Donahue were once partners, Madison knew there was more than a little truth to the rumors and speculation surrounding the man. And the reason behind his cavalier attitude was a well-kept secret.

"Why haven't you ever introduced me to him?" Come to think of it, Madison realized, Kat went out of her way to see that their paths never crossed.

"What kind of friend would I be, throwing my dearest pal to a—"

"Wolf?"

"He has a bit more subtlety than that. You've nothing to worry about. Your kind scares him."

The auctioneer mentioned the next "item" up for bid.

"Then we'll probably see his smoke trail when he hightails it out of here first chance."

Katherine smiled agreement, then slipped beyond the drapes. The crowd applauded.

Dismissing Donahue from her mind, Madison briefly closed her eyes. Oh, Lord a'mighty, she thought. If Daddy could see me now.

The curtain peeled open.

Applause splattered the sultry air, and Madison smiled brightly, scanning the crowd. Crystal stemware sparkled, white-jacketed waiters bearing silver trays moved between the clusters of elegantly dressed people. She didn't know a single one. She didn't travel in those circles. Not anymore. *I bet not one of them could toss a shrimp net,* she thought, absorbing the sea of white dinner jackets and glittering evening gowns. The last time she saw that many sequins it was a corporate party in the Trump Tower. Her practical side thought briefly of how many people could live on the price of her borrowed gown alone. Though incredibly glamorous, it seemed like such a flagrant waste of money. Madison didn't hate the rich, yet she disliked anyone who just hid inside their restored mansions and threw money around to make the problems go away. Katherine was here to see that they threw it in all in the right places.

"After Kevin passed away," Katherine was saying to the audience, and Madison heard the catch in her sorority sister's voice, "I was left with plenty of money but few marketable skills, except how to dress properly and throw a great party. Like this one y'all are enjoying."

The crowd laughed agreement, but Madison knew Katherine had an MBA in business. How did they think she got this far?

"Yet it made me see there were other people out

there in the same predicament, whose skills were going to waste because they were most useful with a marriage license. Wife Incorporated employs mostly women to fill in for anyone who needs those special, and often unrecognized, talents—household organization, grocery shopping, cooking, housekeeping, kid wrangling, sometimes a replacement mother for a vacationing couple, a wedding coordinator or a hostess for a party, a temporary wife for a divorcé or widower trying to get his life back together.''

Madison tipped her head to smile at Katherine, infinitely proud of her sorority big sister. As she had when they were in college, she'd taken the best from bad situations and made them flourish.

''All Wife Incorporated employees are bonded, trained in infant and adult CPR, emergency first aid and self-defense.''

The crowd murmured approval.

Madison and Katherine exchanged a smile forged over years of friendship.

Then the auctioneer stepped up to the podium.

Alex would have bid on her for her face alone.

She took his breath way. Far away. And instantly she intrigued him. Perhaps it was her sable-brown hair coiled loosely at her crown and giving her a sexy, disheveled look—a little free spirit in the middle of tight-laced society. Or the slight disdain in her round cognac eyes as she scanned the attendees. Or the strappy deep-plum-colored gown, saturated with bugle beads, heavy and shaping her every curve. And showing all the really good ones, he thought with pure male appreciation.

Maybe it was that no matter how incredibly alluring she looked, she was off-limits. Wife material. Though, she didn't look very domesticated right now. She looked almost...wild. A sleek cougar with the longest legs he'd ever seen.

The bidding increased, and Alex twisted to look over his shoulder. Brandon Wilcox. He could see the man had ideas of a French maid costume or seeing the woman vacuuming in the nude. Pathetic.

Cookie Ledbetter strolled closer, leaning to whisper, "This is the third function you've attended with Elizabeth, Alex. Are we looking at the future Mrs. Donahue?"

Elizabeth heard and smiled at him over the rim of her champagne flute before taking a sip.

Alex didn't respond, grinding his teeth, feeling as if dungeon doors were slamming shut. A half dozen people had already mentioned that little fact this evening. "Aren't you bidding, Mrs. Ledbetter?"

Her smile was tight before she glanced at the Wife Incorporated woman. "I prefer my help to be a little older and..."

"Less attractive?"

She tapped his arm, smiling kindly. "Shame on you. There is a good reason I've been married to Harrison for thirty years, young man," she was bold enough to say, her expression dancing with innuendo.

"And here I thought it was those gorgeous blue eyes that kept Harry home, ma'am."

Cookie scoffed, inclining her head to Miss Holt. "One does not leave fresh game before a hunter, Alex. And be careful—" her glance slid meaningfully to Elizabeth Murray standing beside him and her voice lowered "—hell hath no fury like a Southern woman scorned."

Alex arched a brow, nodding, and her deed done for the evening, she swept away like Spanish galleon in full sail.

He looked down at Elizabeth and thought how polished she appeared: her neatly twisted blond hair, her flame-red gown, the exact way she stood holding the fragile crystal flute of champagne. She possessed all the qualities he found attractive in a woman—poise, grace, good conversationalist and, above all, she had no inclination to exchange her social calendar for a marriage license. She'd consider the evening a success if a snapshot of her made the latest edition of the *Savannah News Press*. And though he realized it was disgustingly shallow, they both understood the parameters. He knew that after this party was over, she'd either want to spend the night with him or be off to another late-night celebration. She did little else with all her family's money. He just didn't want her to sink her teeth into his. Or demand a wedding ring.

That road in his life was closed. Permanently.

Yet Cookie's comments rang in his mind. Though he'd planned to ask Elizabeth's help with hostessing a corporate party for him next week, their relationship would be blown further out of proportion if she did. He didn't want to hurt her feelings, but obviously he needed to do something. Quickly.

His gaze slid to Madison Holt.

If he won the bid for the Wife Incorporated services, he'd have the perfect solution to defuse this matchmaking society. A hostess with no personal connection. And that's what he wanted most. No attachment. No guilt by virtue of association and making uncomfortable excuses. And Madison Holt, simply by being who she was, was forbidden, and that made her a quick, easy solution.

He made eye contact with the auctioneer and nodded, sipping champagne and wishing it was brandy.

"Alex," Elizabeth said from his side. "What do you need a maid for?"

"She's a temporary wife, Liz. And I don't need either." He set his unfinished glass on the tray of a passing servant and caught Katherine's eye. His former partner's widow, elegant in beaded white, moved across the candle-lit garden and warmly kissed his cheek. Elizabeth inched a bit closer, looping her arm through his. Alex gave it only a moment's thought.

"How's business, Alexander?"

He smiled. She was the only person who called him that. "Not as easy on the eyes as yours, apparently. Do all your employees look like that?" He felt Elizabeth's gaze sharpen on him as he nodded to the woman on stage.

"Madison is special." There was a warning in her tone he didn't mistake.

He arched a brow and upped the bid with a slight gesture. Elizabeth's hand tightened on his arm. Katherine smiled and called him a rascal.

Alex twisted slightly to gather flutes of champagne from a waiter's tray and hand one to each woman, forcing Elizabeth to let go. Another bid aired and he heard an indrawn breath. His gaze flew to Madison Holt and stayed there.

Everything in him jumped to life, and when she shifted her feet, the slit in her gown exposing her leg up to midthigh, his entire body tightened. Beautiful legs, muscular. A guy could get ideas, the wrong ones, and he was certainly indulging in a few. It was sexist, displaying her up there, and she looked as if she'd had enough, her gaze flipping from one bidder to the next as if waiting for her execution. She doesn't like this at all, he realized sympathetically and decided to put her out of her misery. He stepped forward and raised the bid a thousand dollars.

"Alexander, no!" Katherine whispered behind him.

He glanced over his shoulder, noting her concern, then shrugged.

Madison choked, and he swung his attention back to her, trapped by her soulful brown eyes. The auctioneer waited for a second bid. None came. The gavel slammed, and his domestic goddess in plum flinched. He stepped up to the stage and offered his hand. She stared at him as if he'd grown antlers.

"I don't bite."

She scoffed. "That's not what I heard."

He arched a brow, a small smile tugging at his lips. A look of pure challenge.

Madison recognized it and met it head-on. She wouldn't give him the chance to bite anything on her, and despite his ruthless reputation in business and with women, she didn't think his expensive palette had a taste for homegrown. If his date was any indication, he was interested only in her domestic capabilities, and that was fine with her. She had no intention of being one of his conquests.

She accepted his hand, his warm fingers wrapping firmly around hers as she walked down the short staircase to the applause of the crowd. He stood close, close enough for her to feel the heat of his body and his slow lingering gaze. Madison told herself it was the display of bosom that made his look feel like a wolf salivating over a potential kill. At least he's living up to his reputation, she thought, immediately pulling free.

Katherine came to her, giving her a warm hug. "Oh, thank you, Maddy. The Boys Club is going to get a resurfaced pool on that one alone."

"You're welcome, sister," she whispered in her ear, and Katherine's hug tightened a bit. They parted, and she faced Alexander.

Madison had seen pictures of him, but the up-close-and-personal version was a different story. She tried not to stare and told herself that almost any man looked good in a tux. Except this man was the only one in the elegant stone garden wearing black. On Alexander Donahue, the dark fabric fit like a glove. There was no mistaking he was in good physical condition, but then, what else did a millionaire have to do all day? Yet she sensed a bit of rebellion in him, for he'd opted for a white band-collared shirt without the bow tie the other men were wearing. No ruffles, no cummerbund, only a low-slung, black-and-gold, satin-brocade vest that gave him the air of a Southern gentleman.

He slipped his hand into his trouser pocket, hiking up the jacket and enhancing the image of slow grace and privileged dignity. A lock of jet-black hair slipped down to nearly cover one vivid blue eye.

"You're staring, sir."

"So I am."

Madison stiffened. He acted as if he was sizing her up by some invisible standard, and she had the ungracious urge to slap his handsome face.

He slipped his other hand inside his vest pocket and came back with a business card. With a crisp snap, he flipped it over and held it out to her with two fingers. "Be at this address tomorrow morning at nine."

"Tomorrow evening at six," she said, taking the card.

He scowled, a hint of savagery under all that refinement, and she understood why people rarely denied him. She was waiting for the fangs to appear.

"I'm only available during the evenings and weekends, sir. Or did you fail to read the brochure?" She gestured to the slick tri-fold brochures littering nearly every table.

He didn't bother to look. "Apparently," he murmured, and Madison felt his gaze shift over her. It left a smoldering trail.

"If that's not acceptable, then perhaps Katherine can replace me with another."

"No, it's fine." Alex needed her to get started, quickly. The invitations were already out, and he was a little anxious to see if this beauty could do all they claimed. The last thing she looked capable of was anything remotely domestic. "I'm having a party for fifty."

She didn't bat a lash.

"I'll expect you to arrange the catering."

She simply stared.

"And attend as the hostess."

She nodded.

"I assumed you'd want me to hostess that, darling," Elizabeth said as she appeared by his side, lacing her arm through his.

Madison looked on expectantly, waiting for him to change his mind.

"Never assume," Alex said icily, and Elizabeth

stiffened. "And I have to make use of this charitable donation, don't I? Besides—" He patted Liz's hand, the gesture bone dry of sympathy, "you're a guest."

Her look spoke of her dissatisfaction, but it couldn't be helped. Alex needed some separation from Elizabeth and the matchmakers. And he needed it now.

The auctioneer called for attention as a striking man in a white dinner jacket strode center stage. He was a cover model for romance novels, and the charity gift was a night on the town with him. Elizabeth disengaged herself, left his side and started the bidding, sparing him a quick glance.

Alex eyed her, the hint of jealousy in her tight smile, and he was glad he'd bid on the Wife Incorporated services. He motioned to a waiter, and the man brought a tray of pale-pink champagne in crystal flutes. When he turned to offer glasses to Madison and Katherine, both women were gone, only the scent of jasmine and spice lingering behind.

He scanned his surrounding and caught a glimpse of Madison, or rather a rear view. Her beaded gown was slung so low he could see the enticing dip of her spine. She had the sexiest walk he'd ever seen. Alex's body reacted to the delicious sight as she disappeared beyond the stone pillars. He took a deep breath and drained one flute without stopping, questioning his wisdom of getting within earshot of a woman who could command his senses simply by being untouchable.

That, he thought, was more woman than he'd encountered in years.

# Two

*Good God, did this woman look sexy in everything she wore?* Alex wondered, though he hardly recognized her behind those huge, tortoiseshell glasses. In a jewel-green suit with her hair in a tight twist, she projected a competent manner as she strode up his driveway. Far removed from the sleek creature he'd encountered last night. "Are you always this prompt?" he asked, glancing at his watch.

"Always. Consider it a sign of efficiency, sir."

Alex stepped back to let her in, and she swept past. Her fragrance teased, made him think of satin sheets and hot sex. He briefly closed his eyes and shook his head at his own imagination, then let his gaze follow her as she stepped into the foyer and surveyed the area with the practiced eye of a decorator. He knew his place lacked a homey feel, but then, it never felt like much of a home to him.

"Fifty guests you said?"

"Yes." He shut the door.

Madison's gaze jerked to him. His hand in the pocket of dark pleated trousers, he still looked like the playboy millionaire, his tie loose, his blistering-white shirt still holding the crispness from an iron. That glossy black hair dipping over one brow. She was hoping he'd uglied up a bit in the past twenty-four hours, then was glad he hadn't. *I shouldn't go there,* she thought, turning her attention to the foyer.

The inside of the condo bore the same sterile feel of the exterior, out of place in a city where Old Southern charm prevailed. The tile floor was a rich, deep-green, the shade joining the carpet that led up the curved staircase to the second floor. The upper hall was open, offering a view of the foyer below. A massive, arched window directly opposite the front door made a majestic statement, almost bleak when she'd first stepped inside, and now she tried to think of a way to tone it down.

"Come on. I'll show you around."

Following him, they toured through the living room, formal dining room and the kitchen, all rather contemporary, with that antiseptic feel. After inspecting the appliances, which looked brand-new, and estimating the counter space, the need for preparation tables, Madison noticed there were no personal items showing. No family pictures, knickknacks, just a couple of silk flower arrangements, some carefully chosen paintings and crystal ashtrays. Cool, impersonal. Alexander Donahue. She made notes, and as they returned to the dining room with its Queen Anne-style furniture, he pulled out her chair. Smiling, she slid into it, crossing her legs and flipping open her book.

When she expected him to take a seat at the head of the table, he pulled out a chair adjacent to her and sat. Madison scented his cologne, felt the heat of his body, and she sat back to avoid the incredible lure of it.

Alex sensed the barrier between them even at this short distance, and idly he wondered where she'd vanished to last night. Home to a husband? A lover? A cat? Katherine hadn't said, and he hadn't asked.

"Do you have any preferences for the menu?" She shoved her glasses up her nose as she hovered over a huge appointment book, making more notes.

"Can I trust you to select?"

She met his gaze. "Yes. Are these out-of-town guests or locals?"

"Mostly out-of-town."

"And the dress for the party?"

He frowned slightly.

"The attire depicts the atmosphere, sir. May I see an invitation? And perhaps a guest list?"

He rose from his chair and left the room, and while he was gone, Madison studied her surroundings, jotting down ideas and wondering if there was any china in that beautiful cabinet. All she could see was crystal. Very feminine crystal.

Alex reentered the dining room, handing her the envelope.

"After six. Cocktail attire. They'll expect more than hors d'oeuvres. How many have responded?"

"All of them."

Good Lord, she thought. "Famous for your parties?"

He folded his arms over his chest. "It's business. I don't think they'd refuse."

Not if they wanted to keep working for him, she thought, reminding herself he had a reputation for a reason. She focused on her notes, sweeping a loose lock of hair behind her ear.

Even in the dull light of his dining room, Alex could see the rich, bronze highlights in her hair and had the strangest urge to reach across and unpin it, see it fall over her shoulders. He blinked and turned away, feeling her gaze follow him as he moved to the doorway and leaned against the jamb. She kept asking after his preferences, the liquor, bartender, a florist he used. Alex kept staring at her legs, and when she shifted, he glimpsed the lacy top of one of her stockings. He ground his teeth nearly to powder and fought the image of garters and lace and those damned legs and reminded himself that he didn't need to get sidetracked. She was his employee for this party. And he, the paying customer.

"I'll need the key to get in and the hours you don't want anyone around."

He rolled around the doorjamb into the kitchen and came back with the spare key, dropping it into her palm. "The hours don't matter unless its before seven and after ten."

"That shouldn't be a problem. The catering budget?"

"This is the company I used last," he said, slipping a card from his pocket and tossing it on the table. It spun toward her, but Madison recognized the logo.

"Don't care about the cost, then, hmm?" she muttered under her breath, tucking the card in her book. "Have you contacted them yet?"

"No."

She sighed, shaking her head before lifting her gaze

to his. "Mr. Donahue, you already neglected to mention this party was in a week. I have to tell you, it takes more than a phone call to order catering."

"Are you saying you can't do it?"

Oh, that challenge was in his eyes again. "I'm saying next time you want to host a party for fifty, think about how long it takes to prepare for it before you send out invitations."

"That's why you're here," he said with complete innocence. "So I don't have to."

She couldn't help but smile. He really was hopeless.

Ignoring the little jump in his chest just then, Alex said, "Whatever you need is fine, Miss Holt. I'll expect you to be here early."

"Of course."

"Greet the guests, see to the preparations, the servants."

"Certainly. I'll take care of everything, Mr. Donahue."

"Mr." sounded so respectful coming from her, so aging, he thought as his gaze swept her briefly. "I'll assume you'll dress appropriately?"

Madison's features tightened. Did he expect her to show up in thigh-high taffeta and fishnet stockings? "I'll dress the part, Mr. Donahue, if you'll be civil to the hired help." She stood, collecting her book, and with the key in hand, briskly walked to the door.

Alex hurried after her, catching her arm. She jerked around, stunned to find him there, and abruptly he released her.

His gaze searched hers, her irritation confusing him. "I didn't mean anything by it, Miss Holt."

Madison sighed, wondering why that bothered her

so much, then knew his flip comment made her see what she'd known all along—the line between them was wide, her upbringing a long way from his privileged rearing. And he just clarified it. "I know you didn't."

His brow rose, a single black wing against tanned skin.

She cocked her head, meeting his hard, blue gaze. "What kind of man spends two thousand dollars on a temporary wife, on top of the bill for this party?"

His eyes softened, making him look even more handsome, the rat.

"The kind who always forgets something, hates giving parties and would rather have someone else do it, because I'm lousy at it and frankly, too busy."

"Well then, Mr. Donahue, you really *do* need a wife."

She opened the door and, saying goodbye, stepped out and pulled it closed behind her.

No, thanks, Alex thought. That was the last thing he needed. He'd just keep hiring Wife Incorporated for the temporary kind.

The next evening Alex pushed open his front door and heard music. Beach music. And voices, lots of them. Crossing the foyer he headed toward the noise and found Madison in the kitchen, her forearms braced on the counter. In jeans and a dark T-shirt, with her hair braided back, she looked more like a schoolgirl mulling over her homework than an adult planning a party. Another woman stood to her right, the pair listening to tunes on a tape player. And he wondered what the Beach Boys had to do with the party.

As if she sensed his presence, she straightened and turned.

God, what a smile, he thought as she crossed to him.

"Good evening, Mr. Donahue." He looked exhausted, Madison thought. "We'll be out by nine, I swear."

The woman behind her looked suddenly nervous as he glanced impatiently at his watch, then her.

"Perhaps you should go into your study and unwind?"

His lips quirked. That's exactly what he planned to do. He'd considered calling Elizabeth and asking her to dinner, though she'd ream him over the short notice, and although he wanted to lengthen the ties between them, sitting in a restaurant alone was as unappetizing as having to make conversation tonight. He was ready to forego the growling in his stomach and get right to bed.

"Who are these people?" He gestured to the people filing into his kitchen from the back door.

"The staff. They need to know their stations. What I want...et cetera."

"Et cetera," he added.

Her lips curved gently, and she had that patient "I'm waiting" look he'd just begun to recognize. Clearly she didn't want him around, and that was fine with him. He turned toward the foyer and his study. Stepping inside, he found it softly lit, a brandy tipped on the warmer and a meal laid out for him on his desk. The ice still popped in the water glass. Steam rose from the chicken and fettuccini.

His shoulders sank and he dropped the briefcase and fell into the chair.

*I'll be damned,* he thought. He took up the brandy, swirling it to cool, then sipped, loosening his tie and propping his feet up on the desk. He plucked at the salad, popping a carrot slice into his mouth. This, he thought, was nice. Really nice.

An hour and a half later Madison peeked around the edge of the door, calling to him. When he didn't respond she stepped inside, smiling gently. He was asleep, his hands folded over papers on his stomach, a gold pen still in his fingers. The computer screen was still on. She'd done her best to get that meal on his desk when she'd heard him drive up, a tactic to get him out of the way, and was glad he'd done it justice. Crossing the room, she reached across the desk to gather the place setting.

Dishes clinked, and he stirred, his eyes fluttering open. His gaze honed in on her like an arrow to a target. Madison felt trapped. There was something about waking a sleeping man, a handsome man she didn't know, that was terribly intimate. Then he smiled slowly, and she felt heat trip down to her toes.

"Thanks."

"No trouble."

"Why did you do it?"

"You hired a wife for the week, sir." She straightened and turned away with the dishes. "There are perks." Oh, she really shouldn't tease him like that, she thought, smiling.

"And just what are those perks, Miss Holt?"

At the door she paused to glance back over her shoulder. Her look was so infinitely sultry and full of feminine power his body clenched, peaking with his curiosity.

"Aside from the obvious?" She held up the plates.

Her sultry voice gripped him in places he didn't want to think about, and he nodded, unable to find his tongue just then, the images of doing everything but "the obvious" with her crowding through his mind.

"I'm referring to a real wife, you understand."

He nodded.

"Other than two people sharing a life, sharing themselves, making babies and raising them." She shrugged. "I can't think of a thing."

His lips curled bitterly. A storybook representation. Female fantasy, he thought, watching her go, a rather pleasant sight, yet he wondered if she was trying to make him see what bachelorhood didn't offer or luring him in for the kill. Either way, it cleared the dull haze possessing him whenever she was around and made him see clearly. The lady was dangerous to his plans. Wife material.

Like Celeste. Old news, old heartache, he thought, and although the burning in his chest whenever he thought of her had lessened, the lingering sting was a reminder of how blind he'd been. He'd opened himself up more than once, allowed himself to want with a lonely hunger so deep it clawed through his soul, until he found out the hard way those women wanted to be in his life-style, not his life. None of their wants had to do with accepting him with all his flaws. And he had his share. He'd settled for knowing the territory and setting his own boundaries after that. To keep certain types of women on the edge of his life. Women like Miss Holt. Women who offered a glimpse of what he couldn't have. And although his attraction to her was purely physical, it was still a hazard. He was not going to look like a fool again.

Beyond the doors of his study voices faded, cars drove away, and he heard the front door close, the sound hollow in the empty house. He sighed, glancing around, then lifted the snifter of brandy to his lips, feeling suddenly more alone than ever before.

Frowning, Alex crossed his threshold and stopped. Okay, he thought with a look around. The party was tomorrow and this was to be expected. But after a three-day business trip trying to swing a deal that would put his computer division ahead of the competition by two years, he was hoping for some quiet. What he had was chaos. Trucks lined his street. Men carried tables and chairs through the doors as if he wasn't there. The scent of food filled the air. He stood in the high-ceilinged foyer and simply stared. There were plastic runners covering the tiled floor, boxes stacked near the arched window, and the sound of people and dishes echoed from all directions. Alex slung his garment bag off his shoulder, set it and his briefcase by the door, then tossed his jacket on a chair before heading into the living room.

"Where do you want this, Madison?" a tall, muscular man in a tight T-shirt and jeans said. He and his partner stabilized a portable bar on dollies.

From somewhere in the house Madison yelled, "Outside, and be careful of the carpet and tile, David. One mark and I'll beat you up right good."

David and his buddy exchanged a smile and apparently decided her wrath wasn't worth the risk as the two men lifted the heavy wooden bar and carefully maneuvered it through the open glass doors.

Alex walked toward the kitchen, lurching back when two women, looking harried and carrying boxes, darted past, murmuring "Excuse me." Linens stacked the dining table. Glassware, flatware and dishes covered every available space on extra tables. He stepped into the kitchen, the aroma of sausage and onions making his mouth water as he scanned the room for Madison. He cleared his throat.

Seven people looked up and stared as if he might eat them alive.

"Miss Holt?"

An attractive woman barely in her thirties pointed to the back door. "I think she's in the garage, Mr. Donahue."

Frowning, Alex crossed the kitchen, skirting people and counter edges, then pushed open the inner door leading to the garage. A catering truck was parked rear first, dangerously close to his boat. The back was open, the surrounding concrete floor covered with four huge coolers.

He called for her. A clean-cut young man unloading yet another cooler, looked up, inspected him with a quick glance, then inclined his head toward the front of the truck. Alex headed that way, glancing back briefly at the kid as he went around the truck and crashed into someone. Someone soft.

Hands flew to his chest. A cushion of soft breasts and thighs pushed against him, sending him back a step and into the side of the truck.

"Whoa, easy now," he said softly, and in the tangle of their feet, he grabbed her waist to steady her.

Madison looked up and swallowed her breath. She

lay awkwardly against him, his knee thrust between hers. "Oh, my."

Alex gazed into her eyes, thinking a guy could easily get lost in there and go willingly. "You okay?"

"Ah—" she blushed hotly "—yes. Fine." She pushed away from his chest, which only served to grind his thigh deeper between hers. She inhaled, her skin brightening as she scrambled back. His gaze ripped over her, touching on her breasts, then down to her cutoff jeans. She felt stripped naked in the single look. "I do apologize, Mr. Donahue," she managed, then bent to pick up her clipboard.

"My mistake."

His biting tone made her straighten abruptly. "Is something wrong?" She shoved loose strands out of her eyes.

Alex shook his head, looking off to the side as a van rolled to a stop outside his place. His back braced against the truck, he shoved his hands into his pockets, hoping to look casual and disguise his unexpected response to her. "You were going somewhere?" he asked in a dismissing tone.

Madison studied him for a moment, yet when he turned his head and delivered a glacial stare, she arched a brow. "You really should loosen up, Mr. Donahue. You're gonna snap in half someday." She walked briskly away, muttering something about him being tense as a cat on a porch full of rockers.

Alex rested his head against the cold steel truck and let out a breath. Good grief, he thought, trying to control the humming in his body. He could still feel the heat of her on his thigh, burning through his trousers. Just the thought of feeling her warm center made him harder. He was in big trouble if a brush against her did this, he thought, rolling around and heading into the house. In the kitchen his gaze immediately fell on her tanned legs, the curve of her bottom in worn cutoffs as she bent over the oven, mitts on her hands as she lifted out a baking sheet. Scenting the neat rows of puffed pastries, she smiled as she set it on the stove top.

"Why are they cooking here?" he asked, and disliked that everyone flinched. Except Madison.

"They aren't. I am." She removed the oven mitts, and with a spatula, slid the toasted mounds onto a plate, ladled on a white sauce from a pot, spooned on something else from another. She grabbed a bundle of silverware from a stack, laying it and the plate on the work counter. "Everyone," she called. "Take a break." She inclined her head to her crew while pulling a stool to the edge. "Sit," she said to Alex.

He didn't, folding his arms over his chest and watching as the kitchen emptied and she opened the refrigerator, grabbing a carton of milk. The fridge was stocked, two shelves with trays of hors d'oeuvres, and he felt invaded. Felt as if he was losing control over his house. During past parties, which weren't that often, he'd simply asked a woman friend to take care of it and made himself scarce until the guests arrived. It was always quiet, sparse. But this, he thought, was a circus.

"Are all these people necessary?"

"Yes, they are." She poured milk into a glass. "You're the one who wanted to feed fifty, elegantly, in less than five days, Mr. Donahue."

"You did warn me," he conceded sourly. This was his fault, not hers, and it was clear she was trying her best to get it all done in time. Alex wondered if it

was the commotion or the woman who bothered him.
And did she have to look so fresh scrubbed and cute
in cutoffs and that clinging T-shirt?

She faced him, placing the glass on the counter,
then frowned. "Would you prefer your study? The
dining room is being prepared and the—"

He looked at the plate. "What's this?"

"Dinner."

"For me?"

She peered, concerned. "Aren't you hungry?"

"Starved," he said with feeling.

He slid onto the stool and unwrapped the utensils.
He dug into the pastry-wrapped sausage and onions,
tasting a huge mouthful. He moaned, closing his eyes
for second as he chewed.

"Did you make this?"

"Sure," she said, smiling.

He glanced around the cluttered kitchen. "When?"

With a dishrag, she wiped the counter in front of
him. "About a half hour ago. It's rather easy, to be
honest. I was afraid they were going to burn."

That's where she was rushing to, he realized, and
set his fork down, meeting her gaze across the
counter. "You don't have to do things like this, Miss
Holt."

"I know." She leaned on the counter and grinned
devilishly. "It's a perk for hiring a wife." He held
back a smile. "We were going to be in here, so you
couldn't have made anything for yourself and besides,
airplane food stinks and after a six-hour flight...."
She shrugged.

Did none of the women he'd dated do anything for
this man? Madison wondered. Was his life that empty
except for his company? A rather lonely existence.

She knew that every time she griped about her responsibilities, deep down, she thrived on them. What was she going to do with her time, anyway? The age of bar hopping and dating a new guy every week had passed her and even in college, she'd come home twice a month to cook a few meals and see that her dad took care of himself. Daddy needed her more now and helping her younger sister, Claire, with her tuition was a heck of a lot less work than being fifteen with four brothers and sisters and trying to replace their dead mother.

"Miss Holt?"

She blinked, straightening, and realized it wasn't the first time he'd called her. "Sorry."

In that one instant Alex saw her fatigue, a wrenching sadness, and he said, "Perhaps you should call it a day?"

She looked down at her watch and inhaled. "Dang. I still have the tables to..." She left the kitchen, calling for the helpers. He heard rapid-fire instructions, then a burst of laughter. Alex slipped around the edge of the doorway, moving through the dining room and stopping just out of sight. People, mostly young men with rippling muscles, surrounded her, but she didn't seem to notice. He wasn't listening to the conversation, only watching. Something he did a lot around her lately.

Madison gave her instructions, then bumped into him when she turned. "Go eat," she said, pointing to the kitchen.

Alex stared down at her for a second before his lips quirked in a half smile. "Yes, ma'am."

Alex sat at the counter, ducking trays whisking past him, people lugging boxes in and out of his garage and watching her vanish, then reappear minutes later. He hadn't eaten more than a couple bites when she clapped her hands and called an end to the day. She saw the group to the door and Alex found it more interesting than sitting alone in the empty kitchen.

A few minutes later Madison closed the door and faced him. "See. Peace and quiet, as promised."

"I didn't mean for you to railroad them out of here."

"Hey, take it while you can. They'll be back at eight in the morning."

She crossed the foyer, shooting quickly past him and back into the kitchen. He followed like a hungry animal, sliding into the stool and forking a chunk of sausage. "You're a good cook, Miss Holt." Why did his place feel suddenly smaller with just the two of them there?

"Thank you." Her back was to him as she loaded the dishwasher, wiped counters and restored his kitchen, which hadn't seen this much activity in a year, before turning to the counter. She busied herself with storing the remaining pastries in a container, covered them with white sauce, then leaving it on the counter with the lid cocked.

"Let them cool some more, then put the container in the fridge before morning, please."

Alex muttered something, he didn't know what, because he couldn't keep from watching her—her bare tanned legs, her round behind tucked into frayed jean shorts. And while his mind replayed the accidental collision in the garage, his body gave it clarity, thickening as he recalled the sweet heat of her straddled over his thigh. Good grief, he didn't need this, he thought, shoving a forkful of sausage in his mouth.

Alex shifted on the stool, swallowing. "Have you eaten?"

She faced him, her brows drawn. "Yes. We ordered out." She flicked a hand to the stack of pizza cartons in the trash. "Oh, you had some messages." She fished in her back pocket, then laid the stack of paper beside his plate. "Miss Murray called twice, asking if you'd returned. She wants you to call her back immediately."

He didn't, nor did he glance at the messages. He just ate, thinking that in the middle of juggling all her duties, she managed to make him a really nice dinner, yet she ate takeout pizza with the work crew. A woman like her ought to be doing this for a husband, not him, he thought.

"Are you married?"

Her posture stiffened. "I don't see where that's any of your business."

He set his fork down and wiped his napkin across his lips. "You just answered it." And he didn't care for how pleased that left him. Nor how much it warned him off.

She folded her arms over her middle and cocked her hip. "Did I?"

"Women usually let a man know right off."

"If the man is making a pass, sure."

"And if they want one thrown."

Madison didn't like the turn of this conversation. Everything about him felt sharper, blacker, his remote eyes reminding her that she really was a lamb in a wolf's den. She might still have her virtue, but she was by no means man-stupid. And this man had too many women in his past to be trusted on that level. "What are you suggesting, Mr. Donahue? That I've cooked a couple of meals to entice you from your precious bachelorhood?"

His features tightened guiltily.

"Figures." She slid her notebook off the counter, holding it against her chest as she grabbed her purse.

"Miss Holt. That's not what I meant—"

She put her hand up to stop him. "I honestly don't care. Wife Incorporated is figurative. We're not out on a manhunt. In fact, most of Katherine's employees are women who are trying to get their lives back together after being abused by a man." She hitched her handbag strap onto her shoulder and in a cool tone said, "I'd be much obliged if you'd make yourself scarce around here until a half hour before the guests are due to arrive. You'll be in the way. Your usual maid will be here at seven-thirty in the morning to clean, the staff and set-up crew arrive at eight, the catering at noon." She turned toward the doorway, then stopped, glancing back over her shoulder. "You know, Mr. Donahue, you might have more money than the governor, but that doesn't mean poe-dunk to most women when it comes to spending the rest of their lives with someone. And you, sir, can rest easy—" her gaze swept him and found him lacking "—you don't have what it takes to be a husband candidate. Not by a long shot."

She left, and he winced as the door slammed.

Alex plowed his fingers through his hair, then shoved his plate back, wondering if there was a rock nearby to crawl under. Because he suddenly felt like something slimy.

# Three

────────

His mother hadn't raise a cad, and Alex had tried to apologize for his remarks last night by phone. But the number she'd left was a pager. And she wouldn't answer it. The second number was Katherine's, and he didn't feel like explaining himself to her. Kat would call him on the carpet, and he felt bad enough for implying Madison was on a manhunt.

She wouldn't have given her home number, anyway, he thought, adjusting his jacket sleeves. The noise below had lessened, strands of music filling the house. Alex walked to the windows facing the street and flicked back the curtain. He frowned at the sight of limousines in his drive. Leaving his bedroom, he hurried down the hall, then froze at the railing, staring at the foyer below.

He'd swear he was in the wrong house.

The arched window was draped in soft beige fabric.

A vase on the table before it overflowed with magnolia blossoms, their thick green leaves dark and shiny, reflecting the multitude of candles surrounding it. He hurried down the stairs, crossing the foyer and freezing in his tracks. She'd rearranged everything. The living room suite was in a tighter circle with café tables. The sliding glass doors were open and were those his drapes? They were streamed with green ribbon and drawn back with magnolia garlands. Dammit, she was supposed to see to the catering, not leave her mark all over his house.

Scowling, he went to search for her when the doorbell rang. He turned back to answer it just as a young man, one he recognized from the day before, walked toward the door. He waved him off, flinging it open. Elizabeth stood on the threshold.

He forced his features into a resemblance of a smile and said, "Hello, Liz. You look lovely as usual."

"So do you." She swept inside and kissed him heavily, and he had no choice but to accept.

"You didn't call."

"I was occupied," was all he said.

She sighed, her smile a little brittle, and over her head he watched the limousines emptying, his guests marching up the sidewalk. Where was Miss Holt? he wondered, shaking hands and ushering his division heads and business associates inside.

"Oh, Alex, the limousine picking us all up at the hotel was a nice touch," Anna Marsh, a business associate, said and the group around her agreed. "Now we don't have to worry about drinking too much and driving or getting cabs. Thank you, dear, for being so considerate."

Alex stammered for a moment, then said, "You're welcome. The entire purpose, I imagine."

"Good evening and welcome to Savannah." Guests turned at the sound of her voice. "I'm Madison Holt, Mr. Donahue's hostess for this event. Do come in."

Closing the door, Alex turned. His jaw went slack.

"We invite you to come and enjoy the patio. David, our bartender, is there and the buffet is ready whenever you'd like. He can prepare anything you desire, but I would suggest 'Southern Pleasures.' It's a wonderful drink made with fresh Georgia peaches," she was saying, elegantly pointing the way and offering individual greetings as people went by. She was performing her role well.

But it was the woman who had his attention, that and every hormone he possessed.

Oh, she'd dressed the part all right. Elegant, a vibrant splash against the pale decor. Her hair, piled loosely on her crown and spilling down her back in fat curls, enhanced her delicate features, her slender throat. But nothing took attention from the body in that dress and high-heeled sandals. Royal-blue and off the shoulder, it was entirely of lace and hugged her figure. The plunging neckline showed off the swells of her breasts, and the midthigh length displayed the curves of those magnificent legs like nobody's business. He swallowed and had the strangest urge to throw his jacket over her.

"Lovely, isn't she?"

He dragged his gaze from Madison to Elizabeth. "She's the help, Liz."

"Remember that," she said, moving past him into

the living room. Alex scowled at Liz's back and followed.

His gaze slid over his living room, the profusion of fresh flowers and magnolia blossoms scenting the air and filling the corners. The servants moved around the guests slowly, all dressed in dark-green slacks, beige shirts and dark-green brocade vests to match the decor she'd chosen. The buffet tables were gathered up at the corners with blossoms and garlands, and the café tables each bore a centerpiece of edible, sugared fruit surrounded by waxy magnolia leaves. A candle rested in each center, giving the room a soft glow. Yet, the first thing he noticed was his guests were smiling and talking to each other. A rare occurrence, for these parties had a tendency to be rather stiff and brief.

Madison approached him with a tray. "A brandy, Mr. Donahue. Or would you prefer something else?" Like a kick in the teeth, she thought. She'd burned half the night over his comments, ignoring his page, then blamed the incident on the man's notorious reputation of avoiding relationships like the plague and wanting to be aware of his territory.

"Thank you, Miss Holt." That smile didn't reach her eyes, he noticed.

"Miss Murray?" She offered Elizabeth a flute of champagne, her favorite she'd learned from Katherine. Though she accepted, her smile bordered on grizzly, threatening, and Madison decided now was a good time to escape. She immediately turned away to attend to another guest, then stepped out onto the patio.

Alex watched her briefly, then spoke to his guests, Liz at his side.

"Well, I'm impressed, Alex," she admitted after an hour.

He was, too. The entire house and garden had a Southern verandah feel, and it obviously pleased his guests. His usually bland patio was filled with potted flowers and palms, the bar situated under the grape arbor, lit with tiny white lights. Tall torches illuminated the area, adding to the candle glow from nearly a dozen small tables. There was a cluster of wicker furniture that did not belong to him off to the side, where Anna Marsh and Steven Reynolds, a pair who rarely spoke, chatted amiably. With Madison. Her expression was open and animated as she collected up discarded glasses and introduced one guest to another. Laughter filled the garden. A first in a while, he knew, sipping his drink. He made the rounds, crossing Madison's path often, yet she always moved discreetly away when he approached.

When Madison had to address him, it was with a blandness that stung as if she'd slapped him. Yet Elizabeth monopolized his time. As he stepped into the dining room, he hoped the meal might get her to at least join the others. With a quick scan, he found Madison off to the side, explaining the delicacies to over a dozen guests as she handed them each a plate.

"There's shrimp—fried, boiled and stuffed with blue crab. She-crab soup, fried okra, Southern corn bread, spiced hush puppies, Lowcountry boil, stuffed flounder, roasted fresh ham..." As she went on, she told a little tale about the area, flavoring the menu with a bit of history, and his friends, his guests, ate it up as fast as they did the food.

Excusing himself from Liz's side, he moved to

Madison's and leaned to say, "Magnificent job, Miss Holt."

Madison tipped her head to look up at him. "Thank you. We aim to please. Aren't you glad you trusted me now?"

"Yes, very much." He turned toward her a fraction, his gaze lingering over her attire. "You look spectacular."

"Thank you. We manhunters try real hard to lure our prey," she said sweetly, before turning to help serve someone sliced meat.

Alex sighed, and supposed he deserved that, yet realized she wasn't going to give him the chance to apologize. He grabbed a plate, filled it and went off with Liz to eat. The food was incredibly good, and Alex almost wished it weren't. The party was flawless, and he fielded compliments all evening, solidifying his knowledge that he'd made the right choice. He just wished the woman hadn't gotten under his skin.

A half hour later the music changed, growing livelier, and he recognized the Drifters, the Spinners and the Beach Boys in the mix. He stepped out onto the patio to see Anna Marsh and several others dancing as Madison had the servants move the tables aside.

"Does anyone know how to do the shag?" Anna asked.

Madison opened her mouth, then snapped it shut.

Anna noticed. "Oh, you do, Madison, don't you?"

She glanced at Alex, silently asking permission. He nodded, sipping his drink and watched as she took Kyle's hand and instructed him. She was good, getting into the music, yet she didn't linger with Kyle, turning to old man Reynolds and teaching him. The perfect hostess. Anna partnered herself with another guest and soon nearly everyone was on the patio. Madison danced, her sweet behind rocking as she took them through the steps.

The men flirted with her, Kyle asking for a dance over and over, and Alex felt his jaw tighten as she obliged. Liz grabbed his hand to pull him into it, and he hastily set his drink aside and joined. One song rolled after another, and they switched partners. Alex danced with Anna, then found himself in front of Madison.

She started toward the nearest table filled with discarded glasses, but he caught her hand.

She met his gaze. "Surely you don't mean—"

"Why not? Scared?"

Her look said he was a fool for asking. "I'm hired to work, not party till the cows come home."

"And I pay the bills," he countered, stepping closer to slide his arm around her waist and pull her into the dance.

"Not for this, you don't."

He held her gaze, feeling several pairs of eyes watching them, including Liz's. "It's just a dance."

"Do you always use the advantage for your own means?"

Her expression turned sweet, yet he saw the fury lying beneath. "Always." The music was soft and slow, and he nudged her closer.

Her brows shot up. "Mr. Donahue."

"Yes, Miss Holt?" God, she smelled good.

"That's too close."

"All depends on the perspective. And they—" he inclined his head to the guests "—don't matter right now. You're aware I paged you."

"I know. Four times."

"You wanted to humble me."

"Saintly creature though I am, miracles are not my specialty."

Over her head, he scanned his home, his guests. "I would say they were." He looked down at her. "I'm sorry."

She looked up. "Apology accepted."

He frowned. "Doesn't sound like it."

She batted her lashes dramatically. "Why, sah, I'm most grateful and thank you evah so much for concernin' yourself with little ol' me." He grinned, and her expression returned to normal, though hinting sarcasm. "You *were* acting like a complete jerk, you know."

God, he liked her frankness. "Yes, I was."

"That's one for the manhunters."

His lips flattened in a thin line. "I wasn't aware we were at battle."

Madison sighed, mentally chastising herself. He'd apologized, and antagonizing him wasn't going to win her brownie points if she needed a reference. "The South has surrendered, sir. The white flag is up."

He eyed her for a second. "Then tell me, Miss Holt, what the heck does poe-dunk mean?"

"Diddly-squat…nothing. My daddy says it a lot." She responded, smiling. "How come you didn't know? You're from the South."

He shook his head. "I moved here when I expanded my company ten years ago. I was born and raised in Ohio."

Her brows rose. "A Yankee." This was news to her, especially since he had a rather nice drawl.

He grinned, and her stomach flipped end over end. "I'm just chalking up the black marks, huh?"

"I'd give a tally, but the white flag still flies," she reminded him with a smile.

Nodding acknowledgement, Alex sashayed them across the floor, her hand small and warm in his, her body radiating a heat that had nothing to do with the humid Savannah night. She kept a respectable distance between them, yet her hand on his shoulder shifted every now and then, fingertips smoothing the fabric. It soothed, and he simply stared, enjoying the sensation.

"You don't like me very much, do you?" he said.

"I don't know you well enough to make that strong a judgment." Her lips curved. "Let's just say you've lived up to my expectations."

Alex didn't like how much that stung, whether she meant it to or not and he was about to clarify it when the music changed to something quicker by the Drifters. She looked suddenly excited, and the muscles squeezed in his throat.

"This is one of my favorite songs."

"Then we can't let it go to waste." He moved her across the floor to the beat of the music, feeling her reluctantly fall in step with him. "You got this one?"

He flung the challenge with his Irish eyes, and she flipped it back. "Get ready to rock, rich boy."

"You're drawing battle lines again, darlin'," he drawled, then spun her out and pulled her back, rocking with her tight against his front.

"Not bad for a corporate yahoo," she said as he twirled her to face him.

"Are you saying I'm stuck-up?"

"No," she said looking him over. "Just stuck."

He frowned, affronted and confused in the same instance and she laughed in spite of it, liking that he wasn't totally in control and letting him twirl her out. They matched step for step in the intricate pattern before coming together again. Neither noticed as the guests and servants stopped to watch, then cleared the floor as they danced.

And boy, could he. It surprised her, his grace, and she felt weightless as he expertly led. "Where did you learn?"

"I wasn't always a company president."

She gave him her best, do-tell, I-would-never-have-thought look.

His lips twitched.

"My parents were great dancers." He noticed a flicker of pain in her eyes before it was gone. "So are you."

"You too, Yankee."

"I don't consider myself a Yankee, Miss Holt."

"Until you're comfortable saying 'y'all,' 'fixin' to go' and know someone named Bubba, you're still a Yankee."

He laughed, the rich sound rumbling in his chest, bringing heads around as he yanked on her hand, spinning her sharply into his arms and up against his chest. The impact knocked her breathless, her eyes flaring wide, her hands clutching his upper arms. Nothing in her life prepared her for the exquisite feel of honed muscle and man layered tight to her body. Her insides shifted, broke loose.

Only one arm around her slim waist, Alex bent, sliding her low against him to lay her back over his arm for a big finish at the end of the song.

The guests cheered, whistling and applauding.

Alex and Madison stared, trapped.

Every nerve in his body sizzled with the feel of her against him, hip to hip, and in his mind he saw her like this, bowing back as he tasted her rosy flesh, naked and brazen as her sharp tongue. He grew hard and was helpless to control it, knew she could feel it when her eyes flared. Then in a flash of abandon, he wanted her to see the danger of a man like him.

He was ruthless in all things. It's why he owned a multimedia conglomerate at thirty-four. And though she might have all the qualities to make some man a terrific wife, she was right—even if he scraped away the layers, he wasn't husband material. But that didn't smother the animal desire he experienced this close to her. And he was afraid nothing would.

He straightened slowly, gazing into her sultry dark eyes. ''Thank you, Miss Holt.'' He didn't let her go, the contact so hot he thought he'd burn to ashes right there.

Madison swallowed, her body screaming to rub against him, her mouth burning to feel his. ''You're welcome, sir.'' She pushed out of his arms and looked at the crowd, giving them a quick curtsy.

Alex didn't take his eyes off her as she quickly scooped up a tray and collected glasses, stacked dishes. She handed the tray to a server while encouraging others to keep dancing.

''You must teach me that,'' came from his side, and he dragged his gaze to Elizabeth.

''Sure, Liz.'' He swung her into his arms. They danced, unhurried and private, yet in the back of his mind, in a place he didn't want to go, he longed for the feel of Madison, dark-haired and sexy as midnight mist.

* * *

Gradually the guests departed, and Alex felt a little humbled when Madison pulled a basket from the hall closet, handing each guest a gift of local homemade jam wrapped in ribbon and tulle as they left. Her thoughtfulness made this a success, and he wished he could do more than pay the bill. But his thoughts centered on the wrong part of his anatomy when she was around, hazardous territory as far as he was concerned, and he told himself he was glad she'd be out of his life in a couple of hours.

With a wave to the last guest, Madison hurried to the kitchen while Alex stood out front, watching the limos drive away. He lingered, loosening his tie and wishing he hadn't quit smoking and had a cigarette handy. He headed inside, returning to the kitchen. The catering staff looked up from repackaging freshly washed dishes and glasses the instant he stepped inside.

"You did a tremendous job, people. I am eternally grateful."

"You're welcome, Mr. Donahue," they said in unison.

Madison slipped up beside him and he glanced down. He felt drained and sweaty and damned if she didn't look fresh, as if the party was just starting.

She leaned on the counter and, with a look of pure deviltry, handed him the bill.

His gaze dropped to the bottom line. "I didn't know After Eight would do anything at this price."

"They don't. In fact, with the short notice, they wanted nearly three times that." He looked confused. "I used Jasmine Knights on Abercorn." She motioned to someone, and Alex saw the woman he'd met the second day coming toward them. "This is Christine Knight. Her company did all this on such short notice."

Alex shook her hand, praising her efforts, her staff and insisted that from now on, he'd call on her.

"Please do, but try a little more than a week before the event, Mr. Donahue."

Alex flushed, realizing that he'd demanded a lot from all these people.

"That's it for tonight, don't you think, Christine?" Madison asked, and when Christine nodded gratefully, she looked up at Alex.

He motioned to Christine and the women followed him into his office. From his desk he took out his checkbook, a mammoth thing, Madison thought and immediately wrote a check, handing it to Christine.

She blinked at the amount.

Christine left and Madison stared across the desk at him. "The leftovers are in the freezer and fridge in meal packages, Mr. Donahue—"

"You can call me Alex, you know."

Her posture tightened. "I'd rather not."

He shrugged, unaffected, then left his chair, rounding the edge of the desk and resting his rear there. "You saved my bacon."

She met his gaze head on. "Let's be honest, Mr. Donahue. I saved you from letting Elizabeth Murray think she could get her manicured French nails into you."

That brow went up.

"Desperate, weren't you?"

Painfully, he thought, but he wasn't going to admit that to her, and simply stared.

She waved him off, grabbing her purse from the

chair near the door. Alex hurried after her. She was already opening the front door.

"Can I drive you home? It's late."

"Thank you, but I have my ride." She stepped out.

A red pickup truck sat in his driveway, the engine running, the bartender, David, in the driver's seat, smoking a cigarette. Something close to jealousy speared through him. He looked down at her, wanting to say something, do something, and though the urge to kiss her nearly knocked him over, he put out his hand. She clasped it warmly.

"Nice doing business with you, Yankee." With that, she turned and walked to the truck, her handbag knocking against the sexiest behind he'd ever seen.

Alex watched until they pulled out, then turned into the house and shut the door. He leaned back against it, inhaling the lingering scent of magnolias and knowing he would never smell the flower again and not think of her.

But he did think of her. For a week her image, the sweet feel of her against him when they'd danced, haunted him, irritating him. No woman ever commanded his senses so thoroughly, and he tried spending time with other women, any woman, to get her out of his mind. When he managed an entire night without her walking through his dreams, he thought, that was that.

Yet a day later his entire financial world hinged on having a wife.

Right now.

And he could think of only one person who might be willing to play the role.

# Four

"**I** can't ask her to do that, Alexander," Katherine said from behind her desk.

"I wouldn't ask if it wasn't important." Alex was too close to let anything stop him now. He'd worked his entire life to this point—to regaining the company his father had started and been forced to sell in the face of a failing economy and his mother's cancer treatments. Both losses had killed his dad. And a deathbed promise had kept Alex pushing and working until now he had the cash to buy anything he wanted. And he wanted Little People Toys. But convincing Angus O'Malley that his toy company, Alexander's dad's old company, would be in the hands of a reliable fellow Irishman was harder than he imagined.

There was a thirty-day time limit on this sale before it went public. If it did, Alex wouldn't stand a chance against the bigger guns of the industry. He'd already invested half his life for this. Angus didn't have any sons, and his daughters were well married, their spouses having no desire to take the reins. Reins Alex wanted. The time was now.

"I have to consider her feelings in this."

"What feelings? It's fake. For one night, maybe two."

Her eyes narrowing, Katherine tapped the gold pen against her lips. "You are asking her to *lie* to a client of yours so *you* can get a deal." She leaned back in the plush, maroon silk chair. "What happens when the contracts are done and the client learns you aren't really together? It's all a bit underhanded."

"It's taking the advantage. O'Malley is on the verge of sealing this up, anyway. He wants to retire, but he's a die-hard family man. The company logo is 'Happy Families are Our Families,' for crying out loud. He wants to see his employees keep their jobs, and for some reason he thinks my life-style doesn't promise that. Being engaged or married might make the difference to him." Alex hadn't started his own company with a woman at his side, and he hated being judged like that, especially when the thought of marriage made his stomach knot. "He wants the company to grow, and I can make it huge." *And I have to get it,* he thought. *I promised.*

"I don't doubt that, sugah, but this is not the normal Wife Incorporated duties. Madison is very dear to me, and I won't see her reputation ruined because you want to make more money than God." He scowled slightly, and she leaned across the desk. "You are asking her to flat out lie for you. And Madison won't like playacting at all."

"How do you know for sure, if you don't ask her?"

Katherine sighed, sinking back into the chair. "Why not ask Elizabeth?"

He made a rude sound and fell back into his chair. "Elizabeth will have this all over the city in a day, and I'll be walking down the aisle by next week. That's not in my plans."

"Then I was right," came from somewhere behind.

Alex jumped to his feet and turned, his insides doing an unaccustomed lurch as she stepped farther into the room. She stopped a few feet from him, looking too damn good in jeans and a black T-shirt.

"You did take the bid and hire Wife Incorporated to keep her at bay."

"You make her sound like a hound."

"You said that, I didn't." She sent him a smile that read ha-ha. "Guess it didn't work if you're engaged."

"I'm not. Nor will I ever be."

His tone snapped with finality, and Madison frowned, glancing at Katherine. "I thought I heard—"

"You need to discuss this in private." Katherine stood and rounded the large polished desk.

"I don't have anything to talk about with Mr. Donahue. I have to get going, anyway. Daddy needs me."

"Please, stay for a minute and hear him out." Katherine walked to the conference table and poured two cups of coffee from the silver service, then carried them back. "Sit. Talk." Pointedly she met Alex's gaze. "Remember what I said." They accepted the cups and watched as she left the large office.

Then they stared at each other.

Madison set the cup on Kat's blotter, dropped her handbag on the floor, then sat. "Well, do you need another hostess?"

Alex started to take a sip of coffee, then sighed and set his cup aside, as well. Shoving his hand in his pocket, he rested his rear against the desk edge. "No, I need a...fiancée."

Madison raised her brows a bit and listened as he explained about O'Malley.

"You've already told him you're engaged... haven't you." It wasn't a question.

He held her gaze, the look so remote it made her shiver. "Not quite."

Her breath raced into her lungs. "You said you were married!"

He nodded, and inside his pocket his fingers clenched. Angus had backed him into a corner, and that he'd allowed it to happen, with all his experience, was embarrassing to say the least. It was reckless desperation, he decided, but he was facing a thirty-day time limit on fulfilling his dreams.

"You want me to play the role?"

He paused and then said, "Yes."

She met his gaze. "Why?"

Her grilling stare made him squirm. "You're attractive, witty, smart—"

"And none of your business associates or friends know me. Except the few at the party, and that's a memory now. I can be swept away like all the rumors about you."

He let out a short, hard breath, about to contradict, except he knew that was it exactly. "Yes." Though he wouldn't have put it quite that way.

Neither her eyes nor her expression shifted. "Good.

You are not the kind of man I want my daddy thinking I'd even date, anyway.''

He straightened. ''What the hell does that mean?''

She leveled him a frosty look. ''You are a ruthless businessman, Mr. Donahue.'' And that was the only thing driving him right now, she knew. ''And this proves it. Now, I don't cotton to judging people before I know them well, but you come with a lot of baggage, and it ain't pretty.''

Alex glanced away, the lines bracketing his mouth tightening. He'd never cared that others listened to rumor and gossip. In fact, sometimes it helped him, but for reasons he didn't want to examine, knowing that she'd heard the worst of it left a bitter taste in his mouth. But then, it would keep another neat line between them. ''It's all true.''

She scoffed. ''Flattering yourself, huh?''

He turned his head, meeting her gaze. ''Then some of it must be pretty good, huh?''

Madison wasn't going to match wits with him now. ''You do realize what this entails, even for just an evening?''

''I have an idea.'' His smile bordered on wolfish, and her heart skipped.

''Had many wives?''

''No. God, no.''

''Fiancées?''

''A couple.''

This was news. ''Drag them out of the closet when you need them, do you?''

''Very funny.''

She leaned out to take the saucer and cup, then relaxed into the chair. ''You're already deep in the puddin', Mr. Donahue. You'd best tell me what it is you want from me.''

"I want to hire you to act like my wife for one evening, dinner with a man whose company I'm try-ing to buy. After that, its over.''

"Sounds like a one-night stand without the sex.''

"Exactly.''

She sipped coffee, staring at Katherine's desktop, very aware of his eyes on her, his impatience. Let him wait, she thought. It was degrading for him to ask her to dinner and pay her to do it. Did he think she was not good enough to date otherwise, or that this agreement would keep the news of the artificial marriage from leaking to the public? Lord a'mighty, if the press got ahold of this. If Elizabeth did...

"I set the rules.''

"I didn't know we'd need any?''

Her gaze flashed up. "Do you want to convince this man or be two strangers dining with a third?''

"I see your point.''

She set the cup on the desk and stood, taking a step away. "I'll meet you at your place and we pick O'Malley up together.'' He frowned. "It'll make a stronger 'we're married statement.''' He agreed. "I'll prepare a dinner for us.''

"I thought we'd go to the Baintree.''

She made a face. It was posh bistro on the water-front where she swore laughing was not allowed. "Don't take this too personally, but I'd rather not be seen as your flavor of the week.''

Alex had to admire her candor. It was rare that a woman faced up to him. He knew he wasn't the most congenial person, but he was relieved she saw this the same way he did. As a job, an assignment. Yet a part of him, the barren spot deep in his chest refusing to remain hidden when she was around, wanted to be more than a job to her.

"You keep the touching down to a minimum, and no kissing."

His eyes flared a bit. "You're supposed to be my wife."

"I'm frigid," she said, deadpan.

Like hell, he thought.

"What will you tell him later?"

"Hopefully I won't have to say a thing, but if I have to, I'll just tell him we had irreconcilable differences." My life story, he thought, bitter memories threatening.

"Just don't make me out to be the bad guy, okay? Your history has a way of clinging to a woman."

The distaste in her voice irritated him.

"When?" she asked.

"Tomorrow night."

Her eyes widened. "Cutting it a little close, aren't you?"

Hell, yes, it was close, but he'd already recognized that his attraction for her ran too deep for comfort and control, which was why he'd battled over this until it was almost too late. Good Lord, the woman floated through his dreams again last night until he'd stormed through the condo, dumping aging flowers in the trash to get her memory out of his home. And the last place he wanted to be was here, staring into those incredible dark eyes and asking for her help.

"I was desperate," he finally admitted.

"You seem to be that way a lot lately, rich boy." Grabbing her handbag, she headed to the door. "You pay Wife Incorporated directly." She stopped at the door, looking back. "I want to feel like the lady my mama raised and not a—"

"Don't." He hated her even thinking like that. "Don't say it, Miss Holt. I swear that's not what I was thinking when I asked this."

Her expression softened. "I'd like to believe that, but if you'd known me a bit better, you would have just asked and I might have done it."

He pushed away from the desk and crossed to her. "Might?"

She paused long enough to say, "I guess you'll never know now, will you?" Then she was gone.

Alex took one look at her car and said, "I wish you'd have let me send the limo for you."

She didn't need this evening to bring that kind of attention. "I'm perfectly capable of driving myself, Mr. Donahue. Besides, I needed to pick up groceries for dinner." Madison ducked into the limousine, feeling as if she were stepping into a fantasy world.

He joined her. "Don't you think you could call me Alex by now?"

"I could."

His smile was slight as he shifted toward her. "This isn't going to be a battle? Please say the white flag is up."

"Yes, it's up and flapping. We can't have Mr. O'Malley thinking there's trouble in paradise, can we?"

"I realize this is asking a lot of you."

No, she thought, he couldn't possibly know. "I think you could secure this deal without lying to this man."

Her confidence in him startled Alex, then made him

go warm inside. "I suppose, and I don't like this any more than you do, but Angus doesn't say anything he doesn't mean, and his last words were 'if you were settled I'd feel more confident about selling to you.'" He leaned over to an ice bucket and plucked two flutes and a bottle of champagne.

"You make marriage sound like a prison sentence."

"It is." He popped the already loosened cork and poured.

"Your parents divorced?"

He handed her a flute. "They're dead."

Sympathy shaped her features, and she laid her hand on his arm. "I'm sorry."

"It wasn't your fault."

She jerked back. His response was emotionless, unrepentant, and Madison wondered just how deeply their deaths affected him.

"I'd rather not discuss it," he said when she opened her mouth to speak.

She eyed him. "Fine, but when O'Malley asks, you'd better be prepared to speak up." She gulped champagne, then set the flute in the holder.

"I can handle it."

"Lies come easily to you?"

He gave her a dry glance just as his cell phone rang. He responded, pulling out a computer notepad and tapping an entry. He spoke to the caller, then glanced out the window as the limo rolled to a stop in the heart of Savannah.

Madison looked, frowning. They were in front of a rather expensive jewelry store, and before she could question him, a slender, older man left the shop, heading straight for the limo. Alex leaned out to open the door, and the man ducked inside.

Closing the door, the man didn't spare Madison a glance and addressed Alex. "I hope these will be satisfactory, Mr. Donahue."

Alex waved, ending the call, and the man opened a large thin velvet box.

Madison inhaled. It was filled with diamond rings. Diamond wedding rings.

Tucking the phone inside his jacket, he settled back into the cushions and said, "Choose one."

She arched a brow, his uninvolved attitude driving anger through her. He was creating an image, setting the stage, and it stung that the first time she chose a ring with so much meaning behind it, it was for a game so he could own another company he didn't need.

She stared at the rings, so big she'd need an armed guard.

Alex watched her, surprised when she selected a simple, demure band of diamonds, the least costly and ostentatious of the collection. He didn't know what it was about her choice, for she well knew he could afford any one of them, but that particular ring spoke more about her than anything else.

She didn't put it on and lifted her gaze to his. "You select one."

"I don't need to wear a ring." He waved the man off, and the jeweler closed the box.

Madison bent close to whisper, "Either you select a wedding band and wear it, or I refuse to do this." If anything, tonight he'd understand he couldn't pull her into his ploys without sharing the burdens.

Alex frowned at her, his gaze sketching her face

and the tenacity he saw there. "You're going to be a tyrant about this, aren't you?"

"Oh, yes," she said with feeling.

Alex looked at the jeweler, nodding. He opened the tray, indicating the men's rings. With scarcely a glance, Alex pulled the mate of hers from the rows. But before he could put it on, Madison took it from him, slipping it on his finger.

He went still as glass.

A sudden warmth spread through him, her hands soft and delicate against his, her smile Mona-Lisa slight, with mystery, and for the briefest moment he wished this wasn't a lie. He wished he didn't have so much crowding his life, wished he didn't have a well-honed reputation that put her off and made her think less-than-stellar thoughts of him. He wished he was worthy of—

No, he didn't have time for fantasies. He had the deal of his lifetime to secure, and he didn't want a wife, or the heartache that came with loving someone and having them leave. Regardless, he took her hand and watched as he slid her diamond band onto her finger.

His heart wrenched at the sight of it, the circle of water-clear white stones. Possession, it said. A mark for the world to see. His mark. And in the back of him mind, a dark, begging hunger roared to life and taunted him.

"Alexander?"

His head jerked up, his gaze colliding with hers. He swallowed. He'd never heard her say his name. And the whisper of it drove a hard spike of longing through him.

Without pause she touched the side of his face, a

stroke of soft fingers, and Alex nearly moaned at the sweet feel of her touch. Her lips curved, as if she understood all he was feeling. Even though he didn't have a clue.

Her hand covered his. "I won't let you down, Yankee."

They'd crossed an indefinable line, he thought, partnering him with a woman he'd no right to involve in this.

They glanced at the jeweler. The older man smiled endearingly, oblivious to the weight of their deeds. Alex put a finger to his lips, a sign for complete discretion, and the jeweler nodded, leaving the limo. The car rolled away from the curb.

Madison sank into the cushions, feeling drained and accepting the now-full flute. She didn't think she'd experienced anything as elegant as sipping champagne in a limo riding through the streets of Savannah. If only it wasn't a lie.

Alex settled back into the seat, the motion putting him closer to her. He caught a breeze of her perfume, and the same image he'd carried for days flooded through his mind. Long, hot kisses. Wild jungle sex. He shifted uncomfortably in the cushions and tried to redirect his thoughts from her. But he couldn't, watching as she brought the crystal to her mouth, entranced as the pale bubbling liquid slid over her lips. Everything she did aroused him, in the shift of her bare shoulders in the fitted, dark-green dress, the way she crossed her legs only at the ankle. Brown ringlets framed her face, the length of her hair caught in an old-fashioned snood of gold-and-green silk webbing. It fitted her, and he could almost see her in a full gown at a cotillion a hundred and fifty years ago.

Almost. But the images bouncing through his mind had nothing to do with pounds of clothes and old Southern manners, but of bare skin and abandonment. He suspected there was a wild creature under all that delicate dignity.

She turned her head and met his gaze. "You're staring again," she said, and it wasn't at all like he had the night they'd met.

He blinked, then finished off his drink in one swallow. "So I am." He turned the flute rim down in the ice bucket as the limo pulled to the curb.

Alex stepped out, turning back for her. Her legs came first, and as she ducked and rose, it put her smack against him.

Her breath snagged. "I can't walk if you're blocking the way."

He gazed down into her beautiful brown eyes. "There is something we have to get past to make this believable, Madison."

"And that is?"

In an instant his arm slipped around her waist, pulling her flush against his length. Her eyes flew wide, her hands on his chest, her evening bag in her hand.

"Alexander" came in a rush and the sound of his name, husky, whispered as in his dreams, sent him over the edge of his control.

He kissed her, hard.

And Madison came unglued.

And Alex felt ripped apart. It was better than he'd imagined, hotter, sweeter, and that she responded stole every thought from his brain except tasting more of her. His mouth rolled over hers, wet and deep, and she opened wider, her tongue pushing between his lips and making him groan with the pleasure of her abandon. The kiss was raw and blistering, too much for public. Alex knew he shouldn't have done this. Should never have touched her. He was already hard for her and this just made it worse. The urge to push her back into the limo, say to hell with the deal and spend the evening doing just this, nearly overtook him. Then her hands shifted, sliding around his neck, her body laid against his like a layer of silk. He pressed her a bit harder to him, aching in every cell of his body, and a little sound escaped her throat, tumbling into his mouth. And that thought of her being wild…exploded into reality.

He wanted her. Badly.

But he couldn't.

She was the wrong kind of woman for his lifestyle—dangerous even, in all her genteel Southern softness. She was more menacing than Elizabeth could ever be. Because Madison Holt wasn't even aware of her power. And she didn't want a man like him.

He felt lucky she wasn't slapping his face right now.

She wouldn't, not when she couldn't think beyond his mouth moving over hers, his hands sliding down her spine, pausing to squeeze her a bit tighter. Sensations ripped over her skin, telling her this was true passion, devastating her with its strength and the heat gripping her insides. It made her want to be in the limo, in private, and to steal more than the taste and feel and the arousing hardness of him. Yet even as her body responded, her breasts swelling inside her dress, her lingerie clinging to her flushed skin, she knew this was not what either of them needed. It was a game and they were players. Yet that made the kiss

all the more alluring, and she gave in to it, feeling
more like a woman in his arms right now than she
had her entire life.

They heard someone clear their throat. They separated slowly, and each of them, released a long
breath.

"Dang." She stared up at him.

"Yeah," he managed, the incredible heat burning
him still.

She reached up to wipe her lipstick off his lips. "I
hope you don't think that any more than that is part
of the game." She slid her arms from around his
neck.

He frowned, trying to find his breath. "No!" came
for her ears alone.

"I said no kissing. And for a man who didn't want
anyone to know about this, that public display made
heads turn."

He didn't bother to look. "Oops."

He wasn't the least bit contrite, the rat, and she
couldn't stop her smile. Her gaze drifted over his
shoulder, then jerked back to his. "I think this is
O'Malley coming."

He turned, flushing a little as the tall, silver-haired
man walked down the short hotel staircase. He was
grinning.

"Donahue."

They shook hands, and Madison hung back, checking her lipstick and to see if her clothes had ignited.
Briefly she closed her eyes, knowing he'd done that
just to get the unfamiliarity out of the way, ease some
tension, but it didn't work. Her body hummed with
energy, and she reminded herself that this was Act I,
Scene 1. The stage was set, yet the last thing she

expected to feel in his arms was the total annihilation of her senses.

Facing him, she watched the exchange and immediately recognized that Alex respected this man immensely. Madison stepped forward and tried not to flinch when Alex slung his arm around her waist as he introduced her.

"Well, Donahue, now I know why you keep her a secret from the rest of the city."

Let's pray it remains that way, she thought, shaking his hand and noticing O'Malley's gaze drop to the ring. It felt creepy wearing it, like one of those antique poison rings, heavy, carrying the threat of pain.

# Five

Madison felt trapped.

Aside from fielding questions about the lack of feminine touch in Alex's house, where they had met and married, Alex played his role well. Too well. The more Angus inquired, the closer he sat to her on the sofa, the more often he touched her, toyed with her hair, brushed his fingers over the back of her neck. It should have soothed, but it only made her uncomfortable. It was for show, and she knew he didn't want to be doing this, didn't want to touch her.

When Angus left the room to call home, Alex leaned close to whisper, "Relax. You're wound up like a spring."

She couldn't look at him, scooting away and gulping wine. "Then stop touching me so much."

"You're my wife for the day."

"Regardless, I'm not used to being…petted."

"When I pet you—" he growled in her ear "—you'll know the difference."

Her breath skipped, decadent images bursting through her mind. Couldn't he see how hard this was? "Don't say such things, Alexander, please."

God, when she said his name his heart did a quick jump in his chest. "Why?"

"Because…this is just a bargain, not even a date in the traditional sense."

Something speared him then, a wish to turn back the clock. "The bargain doesn't matter, darlin', and you need to be touched all over." He bent closer to add, "And kissed all over."

Goose bumps skated down her throat as she turned her head a fraction, gazing into his blue eyes. Her insides melted under his velvety look. She struggled to remember why she was here. "It *does* matter, because that's all this is. And what I might need is not your concern, not that you would have the first clue." He scowled and she didn't care. She wasn't joining the ranks of his unloved, not when she could so easily fall for him. "You might find this teasing easy, but I don't. I can't keep—" She hated the catch in her voice and swallowed. "Please…we had rules and you keep breaking them."

"We have to make this believable."

"He'd be made of stone if he didn't believe it." Out of the corner of his eye, she saw Angus returning. He made to kiss her, but she put two fingers over his lips. "Don't." She couldn't bear much more of this and remain objective, she thought, yet he kissed her fingers instead, nipping one.

Her eyes widened a fraction, her breath skipping audibly.

Madison looked at Angus. "Forgive us," she said, genuinely embarrassed by their behavior.

Angus waved it off as he sat. "I remember what it was like to be newly married. I must say, I was surprised when you told me, Alex. I'd have thought the newspapers would have spread it over the city."

"Exactly the reason for the secrecy, Angus. We like our privacy. And we'd appreciate it if you'd help keep it."

Angus studied them for an instant, then nodded, saying, "You two need another honeymoon, though."

"We never had one," Madison blurted, then added quickly, "You know Alexander and business." Angus looked disapproving, yet before he could comment, she asked, "So, what's the name of your company?"

Alex stiffened beside her, and she glanced, recognizing the unease in his eyes.

Angus's narrowed gaze shifted to Alex, then back. "Little People Toys."

Madison nearly choked on her wine and tried not to look shocked. "A very reputable company, Angus. You should be proud." There was a faded set of L.P. Toy trucks and dozers in her father's backyard right now for her sister Claire's son to play with.

"I am."

Alex read the message in the older man's glance. He wasn't letting his company go to just anyone. It made Alex want it more.

"How come you didn't know?" Angus said.

"Alex rarely discusses business with me and frankly, after five years in the New York financial world, I don't want to know about it."

Angus eyed her. "I can't picture you in New York."

"Neither can I anymore. I worked for Hughes & Rollins." After receiving her college degree, she'd worked for a large corporation. Although the money had been good, the life-style wasn't hers. She hated crowds and noise and preferred the solitude of the rural area. The country was her home, in her blood, and she refused to fight it.

It only made her unhappy when she did.

It was old-fashioned to want to be a wife and mother and love a family, but just the thought of it gave her a satisfaction the corporate world never offered. Peace in her heart was all she'd ever needed. When Katherine asked for her help starting her business, Madison had jumped at the chance to return home and be closer to her family. She hadn't regretted it for a second. Except she wondered when she would be the lady of her own house, since she'd been the lady of her father's house since she was fifteen.

Alex's brows shot up. Good lord. Mean territory.

Angus whistled softly. "A corporate raider, huh?" he said, oddly amused and stealing a quick glance at Alex. "Aren't you afraid she'll try raiding your stock?"

Madison turned her head and met his gaze. "I guess you should keep me very happy in our marriage, huh?"

Angus chuckled.

Alex stared, then his lips curved slowly as he leaned closer, looking at her as if his entire world rested on her next breath. "I think I know how to please you, darlin'," he said, a willing prisoner in her gaze and for an instant, his surroundings narrowed to the softness in her eyes, the scent of her, her breath brushing his mouth. Without conscious thought, he tucked his knuckle under her chin, tipped his head and kissed her, a light, sweet brush of his lips.

Until she kissed him back.

She couldn't help it. She wanted it. Wanted to see if their first kiss held the unexpected shock of newness, or if this hunger she felt for him was as powerful as she imagined. Unfortunately it was, the hot knot of desire looping around her, snaring her as she worried his lips. Angus chuckled and she drew back sharply, a blush stealing up her cheeks. She wondered how Alex could make her feel both angry and desired in the space of minute.

Angus was smiling like a proud father. "You two definitely need a honeymoon."

"I need to check dinner." She stood and vanished into the kitchen.

Alex watched her flee, frowning. Angus asked where he could wash up and as he headed to the bathroom, Alex stepped into the kitchen.

"You're mad." He braced his shoulder against the kitchen door frame, watching her move from counter to stove.

"You could have told me about the toy company." Madison still couldn't understand why he wanted it when he had a multimedia company. It just didn't jibe.

"And you could have mentioned being a corporate raider."

"You never asked." She slid stuffed capons onto a platter. "Did you really think after graduating with honors, that this was all I could do?"

His features tightened at the verbal slap. "No. Why did you quit?"

"My conscience. My firm bought up stock of a small company and when the results hit my family, more specifically, my father and the livelihood of my hometown, I decided I'd forgotten what was important. When Katherine asked me to help start Wife Incorporated I left at the first chance." She glanced up, frowning. "Why are you looking at me like that?" That stare was too hot to be legal.

"I didn't think anyone could look...appetizing in an apron."

"Angus isn't around. You needn't play the role."

He pushed away from the door and came to her side. "Was that kiss part of the role?"

"If you have to ask, you don't know me at all."

She wouldn't look at him, busy with shifting food into serving dishes, yet he stopped her. She met his gaze. "Was it?"

She scanned his handsome face for the bitterness surfacing, yet she saw only a sweet vulnerability that nearly broke her heart. "No, Alexander. Despite your tactics with Angus, and your numerous failings—" he scowled "—I like you." He smiled. "But then, it hardly matters, hmm?" She pushed a platter into his hands, took one up herself and inclined her head to the dining room.

Alex didn't move for a second. It did matter, more than he wanted to admit, and he didn't like this twisted feeling in his chest. Getting emotionally involved with her wasn't in his plans. The thought of risking that kind of pain again scared the hell out of him. Love was for poets and fairy tales. He'd had his chances and failed. He'd proven that more than once.

They enjoyed their coffee and dessert on the patio until a light sprinkle of rain sent them inside. Angus decided it was time to leave. Alex was anxious for the night to be over, afraid he'd slip up and ruin Madison's hard work. Shaking Angus's hand, he stepped back and was surprised when the older man hugged Madison, whispering something he couldn't hear before she brushed a kiss to his cheek. He marveled at how easily Madison made friends, made people feel welcome as she had the night of the party. Alex felt like an outsider, on the edge of other people's lives. Her life. And though he insisted that's what he needed, wanted, Madison Holt gave him a glimpse of what he was missing. He didn't want to look at what he couldn't have.

With a relieved sigh, they watched the limo pull away, then they turned into the house.

Madison immediately went into the dining room and collected up the dishes. Alex helped, yet not a word passed between them as she put away the leftovers and rinsed dishes.

Lightning flashed beyond the kitchen windows.

Alex stood on the opposite side of the open dishwasher, taking each item and loading them in. "You're awfully quiet."

Her only response was a slight shrug.

His brows drew tight. "Madison, look at me." She turned her head, and the sadness in her eyes struck him like a blow. He frowned. "What is it?"

"I hated lying to him. He's a sweet old man only looking out for his people. And I'm angry with myself for joining in your stupid games."

His features tightened. "Then why did you do it for me?"

"A moment of weakness. You were against the wall and looked so helpless. Heck, I don't know." But she did. Beyond that he was the sexiest man alive and she needed the money to get ahead of her father's hospital bills, she was drawn to him, to find something beyond the bitterness he maintained like a wall to keep everyone from seeing more than he chose. But the real trouble was him. He was charming, a gentleman, considerate of her all evening, showering her with sultry smiles and tender touches. But it was fake. And it hurt. She wished it didn't, but it did. Because every time she looked into his blue eyes, she lost her breath and had thoughts she'd no right to be thinking. Not with a career bachelor. The worst thing was that despite this joke-of-an-evening and her feelings, tonight confirmed how merciless he could be when it came to business. "You're coldhearted to think Angus won't be angry when he discovers the truth."

"He won't. I'll have an affair, and you'll look like a saint."

Her eyes flew wide. "Don't you dare!"

He smiled. "I was teasing."

"Well, I'm not." She yanked off the diamond ring and slapped it into his hand. "Next time you're in a jam, call Elizabeth."

He shoved the ring in his pocket. She grabbed her purse and headed out the front door. "Madison, wait."

She waved overhead, not turning to look at him, though she could feel him racing to catch up. Fishing in her purse for her keys, she unlocked the car door, yet didn't have the chance to slide into the driver's seat before he was there.

He caught the door, holding it open between them. "Wait, please."

"Why?" Overhead the sky rumbled, threatening rain, the wind kicking up and loosening strands of her hair.

"Don't leave this way."

"Why didn't you tell me it was Little People's Toys you wanted to buy? What does a man like you want with a family toy company?"

"That's my business."

She felt as if he'd slammed a door in her face. "Fine. The sooner this night is over, the better."

He scowled. "You didn't look as if you were having such a rotten time."

"I wasn't, actually, until I had to lie so blatantly." Until she remembered that anything he did was a fabrication for Angus's sake. She slipped into the car seat and shoved the key in the ignition.

Unaccustomed panic seized him. "I don't like you driving home this late."

She swallowed the knot in her throat. "I'm a big girl."

"I could call the limo back."

"No, thank you. I've had enough of the posh life for one night." She turned the engine over, yet it wouldn't catch. She tried twice more, and the traitorous thing groaned to a sick halt. She sank back into the seat, staring at the ceiling. "Damn."

"I have a spare bedroom."

"I'll call a cab."

He shifted around the open door and knelt. She could feel the heat of his body and didn't dare look at him. The urge to feel his arms, his kiss, might run right over her good senses. It was clear she didn't have too many of those left.

"This is ridiculous. We're adults. Stay here the night. I don't have to be anywhere till noon. I'll take a peek at your car in the morning." She looked at him, arching a brow. "I am a decent mechanic," he defended. "Getting a cab this late will take another hour at least." The rain fell, first in droplets, then steadily heavier. "Especially in this weather. Besides, you shouldn't be driving. You've had a few drinks."

She wasn't drunk, yet her head was already pounding, and although Madison knew it wasn't wise to be near him, his sincere look almost turned her to mush. Besides, he looked as if he'd stay there, getting drenched until she agreed. She left the car after checking the windows, then ran with him to the front porch. Inside he reset the security alarms.

She immediately went to the phone, then put it down when she saw the time. She'd burn a few friendships if she woke a friend at this hour, yet the thought of her car in his driveway and people thinking she spent the night with him, in his bed, irritated her. Her hand fell away and she faced him, but he was already heading into the kitchen. She followed.

He poured himself a glass of milk, found the cookies and dropped onto a stool. She leaned against the doorjamb. He looked like a kid, dunking the chocolate cookie and jamming it whole into his mouth. It was the fracture in the cold reserve she'd longed to see.

"You're insulting my cooking, mister."

He looked up, chewing. "I had seconds, which were delicious, by the way. Want some?" He nodded to the milk and cookies, intent on his dunking.

"No, thanks. Do this often?"

"Sort of a ritual. Can't seem to sleep without it."

She smiled gently, pushing away from the frame and walking to a stack of napkins she knew were in the top drawer. She handed him one, then poured herself a glass of water before sitting on the stool beside him. She watched him.

Alex was too aware of her, of the curves of her face, her mouth and her body and how incredible both felt, trapped against his own. He kept telling himself he should just ignore it. He'd become damned good at that over the years. Yet this strange feeling, like a fragrance hovering on the edge of his senses, seized him whenever he looked in her eyes. Like now.

"Regardless of what you think, I had a good time, Madison." Her brows shot up. "Angus adores you." He waved a chocolate cookie to entice her.

Madison snatched it, taking a bite. He smiled and her heart did one of those flips in her chest.

"I knew you could be lured."

"Takes more than a cookie, Alexander."

His eyes danced with fresh heat as he chomped into another cookie. "What does it take?"

It was just conversation Madison told herself. He wasn't really interested. "Certainly not limousines, champagne and diamonds, although I'll admit that was fun."

"Are you saying you don't care about money?"

"Not in the sense that you do." He looked curious. "Well, look at this place." She gestured to the expensive condo, the priceless artwork covering the walls. "When is enough? When are you going to enjoy it? 'Cause, honey, you can't take it with you. And alone, it's just...stuff."

"It's my stuff. I worked hard for it."

Now he looked like a little boy defending his end of the playground. "I know, be proud of it. I would. But are you happy, Alexander?" His features shifted with confusion. "Kat told me how hard you work, how you keep expanding, but when will you enjoy it?" Her gaze narrowed sharply, suddenly. "And I swear, if you pull apart O'Malley's business and sell it off, I will never speak to you again."

"What I do with it is not your concern."

She was meaningless in his schemes, she thought, hurt. "Fine. You're right. We've already been over this." She put up a hand. "And before you get all indignant, let's just drop it." She left the chair. "I'm the hired help."

He shot off the stool, catching her by the arms. "Why do you keep saying that? Good Lord, I don't think of you as the help."

"Then what do you think of me?" Her breath snagged as she waited.

His gaze raked her heavily, lushly. "Forbidden territory."

Her insides tingled. "Why?"

"You're wife material. A good girl."

She shoved off his touch. "And you prefer the bad ones, the trash? You don't have much self-esteem, do you?"

He shrugged. "I know where they stand and where I do."

She stepped closer, gazing into his blue eyes. "Oh, Alexander," she whispered. "Who hurt you so badly?"

The compassion in her eyes weakened him, slayed him, and his determination not to fall vulnerable to it made his voice harsh. "No one but my own gullibility."

"We all get hurt once in a while. A broken heart is the only thing we can't protect ourselves from."

Alex snickered bitterly, looking away. "I can." He wasn't getting into this, not with her. It was only curiosity, he told himself. He didn't wonder why women wanted no more from him than a piece of his lifestyle; he'd made it clear his heart wasn't in the bargain. A good time and that was it. He met her gaze, thinking that she understood, and, he reminded himself that they were as ill-matched as oil and water, but it didn't comfort him. It just made him feel hollow inside.

"Want to talk about it?"

He met her gaze, fighting the temptation. "Looking for gossip validation?"

"There are people who couldn't care less, you know," she said crisply.

"You believe it."

The uncertainty in his voice didn't escape her. "Not everything," she offered honestly. "But I've seen you in action, and asking me to playact for you doesn't offer much of an argument on your behalf."

"I won't defend myself."

"I'm not asking you to. I was just a pair of ears ready to listen."

She made it all sound so simple, he thought.

When he didn't answer she said, "So, where do I sleep?"

With me, he wanted to say, aching to take her in his arms right now. Almost needing it. What he wouldn't give to love her for a little while and safely walk away without heartache. But Madison was a woman no man could ignore—ever. She'd already left her indelible impression under his skin, and that was dangerous enough. "Third door on the left."

She turned away. Alex lagged behind, not daring to get too close or he'd drag her into his arms for a kiss he knew she didn't want. When she reached the upper stair landing, she looked down where he stood in the foyer.

"I still think you could have sealed the O'Malley deal without me."

He folded his arms over his chest, half resenting her comments and half enjoying too damn much that she had so much confidence in him. "We'll never know, will we?"

Sighing, she shook her head. "I hope you get what you want, Alexander. Good night." She slipped into the room and closed the door, sagging against the wood. Such a wounded soul, she thought, and though she wanted to understand, he was never going to let her meet his demons. He wasn't going to let anyone that close without a fight.

# Six

Stepping out of the shower, Madison towel dried her hair, then herself. It was late and she wanted out of here before the world started speculating over her car in his driveway. Wishing she'd asked Alex for a bathrobe, she wrapped herself in the towel, crossing the bedroom to her clothes.

Before she reached them, a soft knock rattled the door.

Quickly she searched the room for the flannel shirt he'd given her last night. But she couldn't find it. She crouched to look under the bed. Nothing.

The rap came again. "Hold your horses, tycoon." Securing the towel, she opened the door a few inches, peering around the edge. She scanned him from head to scuffed work boots, pausing on the dirt and stains dotting his green T-shirt and worn jeans. This was a switch, she thought.

He smiled. "Good morning."

"I overslept, my head is pounding. It's not a good morning." He kept smiling and her irritation softened a little.

"Maybe this will help?" He held a mug of coffee.

Clutching the knotted towel at her breasts, she opened the door a bit farther and accepted it, taking a sip. Light cream, no sugar and she was touched he'd remembered.

"And this?" Two aspirin lay in his palm.

She tossed them back with a sip of warm coffee, then eyed him. "You're just full of help this morning."

He reached into his back pocket, coming back with a packaged toothbrush. "Thought you'd need this, too."

She took it, studying it like a puzzle. Her gaze shifted to his. "Keep an ample supply of them for all those overnight guests, do you?"

His smile thinned. He inched closer, taking the mug and stealing a sip of her coffee. It seemed the most natural thing to do. "No, I picked it up this morning with the raspberry Danish and motor oil."

Her eyes widened. "You're trying to fix my car?"

"Almost done. Except I have to jerry-rig the alternator. The auto-parts store was out of your make and model. I'm afraid there are parts all over my driveway right now."

Stepping into the hall, Madison glanced beyond him to the front door, which stood wide-open. Though she couldn't see her car, she suspected it was jacked up and crying for a real mechanic. "Alex," she groaned, letting him have the mug again. "David could have fixed it."

''Trust me,'' he said into the cup.

''You're management, not labor.''

He shifted closer, his voice low. ''I haven't always been, you know.''

The heat of his body lured, and she reached, rubbing a grease smudge from his cheek. ''What did you do before your success?''

''Everything from pump gas to construction.'' He leaned, his face near as he set the mug on the wall rail behind him. She scarcely noticed. ''They don't put that in the papers.''

''Somehow I don't think you let them.''

He grinned and her insides went tight with quick hunger. ''I need to get dressed.''

His gaze slid warmly down to the edge of the towel, then lower. He inhaled through clenched teeth. ''I kinda like the way you are, darlin'.''

''Alexander,'' she scolded, and Alex came unhinged, advancing, backing her against the papered wall. She blinked up at him, gripping the towel. ''This isn't wise and you know it.''

He braced his hands on the wall beside her head, his body a warm shield against the conditioned air floating around them. ''Do you always look this good in the morning?''

Heat spun through her. ''Coffee, aspirin, a toothbrush and now flattery?''

His brow knitted. No one told this woman how sexy she was? ''I mean it.'' His gaze swept her. Her damp hair was curling, framing her face, falling over her shoulders. Bare smooth shoulders. She looked good enough to eat.

And he was hungry.

Suddenly he covered her mouth with his, touching

her only there, his lips hot and rolling. She opened
wide for him, one hand rising to cup his jaw. It made
him feel helpless, showed him she was not as immune
to the passion they shared as he'd thought. His tongue
pushed between her lips, and a little sound broke in
her throat. He drank it, absorbed it like a thirsty soul.
This wasn't what either of them needed, but it was
what they wanted. He could tell by the way her lips
devoured his, her body arching away from the wall
to get closer to him. She wasn't the woman for him,
no woman was, but Madison had a drugging feminin-
ity unmatched by any woman he'd ever known. He
wanted to explore this, see what it was about her that
truly drew him. He barely slept last night thinking
about it.

Yet Alex knew one thing. If he kept kissing her,
he'd carry her into the bedroom and make wild love
to her. And it would be wild. Burning and slick and
sweet. It was already tearing through him.

He toyed with her mouth, nipping her lower lip,
and she repaid him, cupping his jaw in both hands
and holding him for her kiss. Alex groaned and
mashed her against the wall, his arms wrapping
around her waist and dragging her tightly to him.

Madison gasped at the solid feel of his length
against her, and he stole the chance to taste the line
of her throat, the swells above her breasts. Her hands
stroked his shoulders, his hair, and she tipped her
head back, the place between her thighs slick with a
throbbing ache, and she thought she'd come apart
when his hands dove beneath the towel to cup her
bare buttocks. She inhaled, and he thrust against her,
letting her feel every hard inch of him, and she knew
she'd created it.

She trembled, touching, kissing, feeling all there was of him. "Alexander."

"Yeah, darlin', I know."

"We can't do this—"

He kissed her into silence. "We are."

"Would you stop if I asked?"

"Yes." He licked a path to her breast and thought of honey and warmth. "Are you asking?"

"I...don't rightly know."

Her fingers deepened into his hair, and his hunger grew.

His name on the air and hurried footsteps penetrated the haze too late. Alex straightened abruptly, shielding her as he turned to face Angus O'Malley who was already through the open front door.

"Forgive the intrusion."

Alex gawked. "Angus!"

Madison inhaled, crouching behind him. This can't be happening. Oh, if her father knew she was trapped like this she'd be skinned alive. Even at her age.

"What are you doing here? We weren't meeting till noon, right?" He took a step.

"Be still! He'll see me!" she whispered heatedly.

Angus cleared his throat, smothering a smile. "I was right to come by, then. You two do need a honeymoon."

"Oh, Lord save me," Madison moaned behind him, her face buried in his back. She tried inching toward the bedroom door, but Alex wouldn't budge.

"I spoke to Laura this morning, and she insisted I extend an invitation to our summer house on Lake Michigan. We're renewing our wedding vows after forty years, and I'd love you and Madison to come join us. Laura is looking forward to meeting you, and well, we'd like to get to know you better.''

*If I decide to sell Little People to you,* he was saying.

"Tell him," she hissed from behind before dragging him with her to the bedroom and darting inside. She slammed the door.

Alex flinched, righting his shirt.

He glanced between Angus and the sealed door.

How the heck was he going to get out of this without destroying his chances to buy the company and without hurting Madison?

He had a sick feeling this lie was going to cost him more than just cash.

Alex rapped. "Madison, darlin'."

She flung the door open, pinning him with a hot glare. "Don't you dare *darling* me, Alexander." She adjusted the shoulder of her cocktail dress.

"Sorry. I was supposed to meet Angus later."

"I knew I should have hitchhiked home." She jammed on her heels, pushing past him out the bedroom door. "I have never, in my life, been so embarrassed. No, don't touch me," she snapped when he reached for her arm. Then she marched down the stairs.

"There was nothing untoward. Your reputation is safe. He interrupted a man and his wife."

"Two seconds more," she muttered, "and I'd have been buck naked and begging."

"I thought you were close to that."

She sent him a viperous look as she met the bottom step. "Drop dead, Yankee."

Suddenly he caught her around the waist and

dragged her up against him. Madison wrestled with him for a second, then sighed, staring at his chest.

"Are you going to ignore what almost happened up there?"

Her head jerked up. "No. Yes, I am. *I am*," she said as if she'd suddenly come to a life-altering decision. Those moments outside the bedroom were just a stopover in his plan to stay single till death. A hot flush shot through her, the very memory of this man's mouth on her body stirring her senses beyond belief, and she knew if they hadn't been interrupted, she'd have gladly let him do whatever he wanted.

And she would have had to live with the consequences. She'd kept her virtue this long by sheer lack of opportunity, yet she wasn't about to let it go lightly. "It was a weak moment. Given to lust."

He frowned, a little hurt. "It was more than that."

"Doesn't matter now, does it?" She pushed out of his arms. "You've had nothing but casual relationships for so long you wouldn't know the real thing if it slapped you."

His frown turned menacingly dark. "Dammit, Madison, that's unfair."

"What are you going to say? That after a few days you're ready for monogamy that'll last longer than a day?" His chilling expression spoke volumes. "I rest my case." She turned toward the door.

He blocked her path. "I've worked my entire life for this deal, Madison. I can't lose it now."

"It's your problem. I did my part." She shifted around him. "You tell Angus we're not married or engaged, that we are...nothing." Her voice broke a tiny bit, and she hated it.

"I can't. I won't. We're in this together now."

She rounded on him, in his face. "No. One night, you said. I will not go to Michigan, of all places, and pretend to be your wife for Lord knows how long."

"A week, maybe more."

"Forget it."

"I'll pay you." Her eyes flew wide. "Five thousand."

She brought her hand up to slap him, but stopped short, closing her fingers and lowering her arm. "You're completely heartless, Alexander," she choked. "Not everyone is ruled by money and power." She spun and walked out the door.

Alex clenched his fist, his insides twisting. Desperation clawed at him. He already knew her. If she left, he wouldn't see her again. She wouldn't answer his calls, wouldn't even acknowledge him if they met on the street. And he couldn't bear it. He didn't deserve her help, yet all his resolve and rules crumbled away when she crossed his threshold.

"I'm sorry." She kept walking. "Madison!"

She stopped, her back to him. "Gentlemen do not shout."

"I thought Southern women were supposed to be amiable. But you're the most stubborn female I've ever met," he said as he crossed to her, gripping her arms when she looked as if she'd bolt. He pressed a kiss to her forehead, briefly closing his eyes. "I'm sorry. I didn't mean to insult you, I swear. God, I can't do much right around you." He laughed mirthlessly and felt her relax slightly. "Be reasonable. It's raining. Your car isn't running, and the entire neighborhood is getting an eyeful of our business. Come back inside and talk to me."

She glanced, then sighed. "Fine. Call me a cab,

then.'' Pushing out of his arms, she went back into the house. But she wasn't staying. She couldn't do this, not and wonder whether every time he touched her, it was for his plans or for himself.

"I'll take you anywhere you want, later."

She gave him a condescending look. "I have a life, you know." She glanced at her watch. "And part of it starts in less than two hours."

He frowned, closing the door, tempted to lock her in. "What are you doing on a Saturday?"

"None of your business," she said, striding to the kitchen. "You're going to have to tell him, Alex."

"Not until the papers are signed."

Grabbing the carafe, she paused to look at him. "Can you do that? Legally?"

"My personal life is not part of the contract."

She scoffed, pouring a cup for both of them. "Apparently it's a major factor, if you're willing to go to this extreme."

"It got out of hand, that's all."

"Alexander," she began patiently, bringing the mugs to the breakfast counter and sliding onto the stool. "Me going along to Angus's home as your *bride*," she enunciated and watched him cringe, "is just the start of your troubles."

He knew that. Too well. He couldn't decide whether this mess was hurting or helping him. The thought of spending two weeks with her in close confines excited and scared him. She was a good woman, with scruples and honor and self-worth. And he knew he had to open up to her, give parts of himself he hadn't shown anyone since his parents died. Madison would accept no less.

"Are you, at least, ready to discuss this, hear my

side?'' He would tell her only the minimum, he decided. She didn't need to know how much of a fool he'd been with Celeste.

Elbows braced on the counter, Madison stared over the rim of the mug. "I won't change my mind." Then she noticed one thing. Although she'd given back the diamond ring, he still wore his.

The plane arrived on time, despite the rain out of Savannah.

The first-class flight and the limousine ride to the inn should have eased Madison's misgivings about Alex, but only made her see why women flocked to him. It was the life-style. And it wasn't hers. Not that the royal treatment wasn't nice, but it was meaningless to her. And he'd been conducting business the entire flight, fielding phone calls, sending faxes and e-mails from his laptop. He seemed suddenly frantic there for a while, but asking about it only got her an "it's business" response. The man never relaxed, never ceased checking on the progress of this project or that, as if nothing could be done without his final touch. Why did he have all those executives, if he didn't trust them to do their jobs?

He appeared perfectly comfortable with faking a marriage. She thought it was the biggest mistake of her life. Everything in her screamed she would come out the loser, yet once he'd told her about his deathbed promise to his father to regain the toy company, she'd capitulated, softening for him and his story. She wished she didn't understand, but she'd made a similar promise to her mother hours before her death. It's what kept her from living too far from her family in case they needed her, and kept her working for Wife

Incorporated and Jasmine Knights to help with the bills. But like her mother's request, his father's was too much to ask of a teenager just learning about himself.

Alex nudged her, and she glanced first at him, then to the staff member standing outside their hotel room door.

The young man flung the door open. "Welcome to River Winds, Mrs. Donahue."

*Mrs. Donahue.* Oh, Lord. She stepped inside, glancing at the accommodations.

The odds were stacked against her.

Angus had made the reservations, the only ones left in any hotel for miles because of a local festival, they'd discovered. And theirs was a suite. The honeymoon suite.

Okay, she was a big girl. She could handle this. She tossed her purse on the sofa and, ignoring the huge four-poster bed, crossed the living room to open the balcony doors. She inhaled, stepping onto the wooden deck. "Oh, Alex, come look at this!"

The view was breathtaking—the blue lake and lovely homes hemming the shore. The inn was on a hillside, overlooking a street leading to the water, and instantly she felt the tension slip away. Closing her eyes she tipped her face to the warm sun. *Okay, this isn't so bad.*

"Alexander?"

He didn't respond, and she peered into the suite. He was pacing, the phone to his ear as he tipped the bellman. As soon as the young man left, he shrugged out of his raw-silk sports jacket and slid behind the small desk.

Madison let out a shrill whistle. He winced and looked up.

"Were you born with that stupid thing stuck to your ear?"

He muttered something into the cell phone and disconnected, yet he didn't put it away.

"This isn't going to work." She went out onto the deck.

Alex rushed after her. "It will."

Her back to the view, her elbows braced on the rail, she eyed him. "I know this is a real stretch for you, but we're supposed to be married, *newly married.* And a husband who faxes before the plane takes off, takes calls during a lobster lunch and ignores his bride—" she enjoyed the little jerk in his shoulders when she clarified that "—will not convince Angus. I'm not sure we did the other night."

His lips quirked, his gaze slipping over her from head to foot and leaving a warm trail on her skin as he moved up beside her. "We did in the hallway." He propped his forearms on the rail. He leaned closer.

She held him back. "No funny business."

"Depends on what kind." He pushed into the pressure of her hand on his chest and brushed his mouth over hers.

"That kind."

"I make no promises." His hand slid warmly over her stomach, fingers curling around her waist. Her muscles flexed under his touch.

"Alex," she warned, although she kissed him back, let him pull her close.

"I can't hide that no matter what, I want you." He felt her indrawn breath as his lips worried hers. "I want you, Madison."

Her heart soared, then dropped like a stone. "But for how long is the problem."

He stiffened and leaned back, his brows furrowed. "I can't give you what you want."

Her smile was sad. "Then neither can I."

"I didn't ask you to come with me so I could seduce you."

Her expression softened. "Oh, Alexander, you don't even have to try."

Neither did she, Alex thought. Just being near her made him feel more alive than he had in years. His gaze slid over her, the tailored white slacks, lemon-yellow blouse and navy-blue collarless jacket. She looked polished and elegant. But it went deeper than that, he knew. She was so damned sexy he could scarcely think straight, and he would like nothing more than to drag her into his arms and kiss the daylights out of her.

He'd probably get slapped for sure then.

"Can't we just let things...happen?"

"Gee, what a risk for you. Sure you're up to a real friendship?"

Suddenly he slid his fingers along her jaw, staring deep into her eyes. "I know my mistakes got us into this, and I'm sorry. I'll take care of O'Malley, but all I ask is that you just be yourself with me. No bargains, no reporters, no Wife Incorporated, just be with me."

There was something in his eyes just then, a fear Madison had never thought to see, a pleading that had little to do with regaining a toy company. The sight of it lanced through her soul, the same look when he'd told her about his mother withering away from cancer, his father dying only weeks later and leaving him alone. Though he'd been evasive about what happened to him after their deaths, Madison could only assume he'd lived in foster homes. Yet the loss scarred him deeper than he wanted anyone to know. Loveless, discarded. Fiercely determined to succeed where his father had failed. He'd shown her a small part of himself, and with the truth had come admiration, for his success and the struggle he'd endured to gain his wealth and power. By grit and sweat. Most people thought he'd had a privileged upbringing, herself included, and the shared secret endeared him more to her, made her want to find another crack in the iron shield around him.

"What do you say? Though you'll need this." He held up the diamond band, then took her hand, sliding the ring on her finger. "Be my wi—"

"Don't say it," she cut in, pulling free. She couldn't bear hearing him say those words. This marriage was still artificial, his last desperate measure to fulfill his father's final wish. It was the only reason she'd agreed, she swore. Then she knew that was a lie. She was already in danger of falling for him. "No expectation," she said lightly. "Let's just say we'll put our differences on the back burner for this."

"A truce?"

He looked wonderfully eager, and her lips twisted wryly. "White flags are flying, Yankee."

His eyes soft, he leaned, brushing his mouth over hers. "Thank you, Madison."

His kisses felt too good. "Sure you can fake being husband material?"

His smoldering gaze swept down her body. "There's one duty I don't think either of us would have a problem fulfilling."

''*That's* not up for debate,'' she muttered, gently pushing him back.

Ducking close he whispered in her ear, ''I remember what your bare behind feels like in my hands, what your breasts taste like beneath my tongue.'' He adored the little helpless sound she made, the way she gripped his arm, and Alex wondered why he was torturing himself like this. She was pure temptation.

She tipped her head to meet his gaze. ''That mouth should be outlawed.''

His smile was slow and bone-melting sexy. ''I said I didn't bring you with me to seduce you.'' His tongue swept over her lower lip, eliciting a tiny gasp. ''I didn't say I wouldn't try.''

''Failure is imminent.'' But not if he kept that up, she thought, and almost begged him to keep going and take the choice from her. ''Do try to behave, please.''

''Uh-uh,'' he murmured against her lips. ''I can't resist taking the advantage.''

Alex kissed her, as he'd wanted to from the first moment he'd laid eyes on her. Slow and wet and soul-wrenchingly hot. And an incredible feeling spread through him when she gripped his shirtsleeves, giving and taking. Hungry, wild and womanly soft. Just the knowledge that a woman like her let him touch her and wanted more tore him in half. His cell phone rang, and they parted, breathing heavily, and when he turned away to answer it, his knees shook. Alexander realized this was one ride he couldn't walk away from without injuries. The suite, the privacy, was dangerous ground. One look at her, one flash of an image of her in that bed with him, so near, and for the first time since he was fourteen, angry and behind bars, he was afraid this was one mistake he'd never survive.

## PLAY THE
# Lucky Key Game
## and ge

## HOW TO PLAY:

1. With a coin, carefully scratch off gold area at the right. Then check the claim chart to what we have for you — **FREE BOOKS** and a **FREE GIFT** — **ALL YOURS FREE!**

2. Send back this card and you'll receive brand-new Silhouette Desire® novels. These books have a cover price of $3.75 each in the U.S. and $4.25 each in Canada, but th are yours to keep absolutely free.

3. There's no catch. You're under no obligation to buy anything. We charge nothing — ZERO — for your first shipment. And you don't have to mak any minimum number of purchases — not even one!

4. The fact is thousands of readers enjoy receiving books by mail from the Silhouette Reader Service™ months before they're available in stores. They like the convenience of home delivery and they love our discount prices!

5. We hope that after receiving your free books you'll want t remain a subscriber. But the choice is yours — to contin or cancel, any time at all! So why not take us up on our invitation, with no risk of any kind. You'll be glad you dic

# YOURS FREE!
## A SURPRISE MYSTERY GIFT

We can't tell you what it is...but we're sure you'll like it! A
# FREE GIFT—
just for playing the
LUCKY KEY game!

# FREE GIFTS!

## NO COST! NO OBLIGATION TO BUY!
## NO PURCHASE NECESSARY!

**DETACH AND MAIL CARD TODAY!**

## PLAY THE
## *Lucky Key Game*

Scratch gold area with a coin.
Then check below to see the gifts you get!

# YES! I have scratched off the gold area. Please send me the 2 Free books and gift for which I qualify. I understand I am under no obligation to purchase any books, as explained on the back and on the opposite page.

**326 SDL CYAH**                                              **225 SDL CX99**

Name
_____
(PLEASE PRINT CLEARLY)

Address _____ Apt.#

City _____ State/Prov. _____ Postal Zip/Code _____

| | |
|---|---|
| 2 free books plus a mystery gift | 1 free book |
| 2 free books | Try Again! |

Offer limited to one per household and not valid to
current Silhouette Desire® subscribers.
All orders subject to approval.

**(S-D-01/00)**
**PRINTED IN U.S.A.**

# The Silhouette Reader Service™ — Here's how it works:

Accepting your 2 free books and gift places you under no obligation to buy anything. You may keep the books and gift a
return the shipping statement marked "cancel." If you do not cancel, about a month later we'll send you 6 additional no
and bill you just $3.12 each in the U.S., or $3.49 each in Canada, plus 25¢ delivery per book and applicable taxes if any
That's the complete price and — compared to cover prices of $3.75 each in the U.S. and $4.25 each in Canada — it's q
a bargain! You may cancel at any time, but if you choose to continue, every month we'll send you 6 more books, which
may either purchase at the discount price or return to us and cancel your subscription.

*Terms and prices subject to change without notice. Sales tax applicable in N.Y. Canadian residents will be charged
applicable provincial taxes and GST.

# Seven

The eighty-degree heat and mosquitoes didn't seem to bother the children. Or Madison, Alex thought, watching as she helped one of Angus's grandchildren into a swing, then guided a second down the small slide. Clad in white shorts and a purple cotton shirt, her hair braided back, she looked cheerleader cute, and when she glanced up, meeting his gaze across the yard, Alex felt rewarded by her smile.

They'd arrived in time for an early dinner, casual and noisy, and she fit in with the large group easily. He admired that about her, her quick comfort with strangers when he felt on edge, wishing he had a few minutes alone with Angus. But the older man avoided any talk of business, and after a while Alex gave up. Around him Angus's three daughters and their husbands either lounged in chairs on the porch, watching their kids, or helped clean up after the meal.

"Bridgett," Madison called, walking close, yet keeping her eyes on the kids and the shore. "They want to swim."

Bridgett groaned, pushing herself out of the chair.

"No, rest. I'll take them in," Madison offered.

Angus's eldest daughter blinked. "I can't ask that."

"You didn't. I offered." She looked at the other mothers. "Suzanne and Paul can swim, right?" They nodded, and she smiled, turning to the children, gathering up the toddlers and whistling for the others. Alex laughed to himself as she herded the half dozen children into the house to change. Ten minutes later five children, Madison carrying a sixth, were running to the tire swing hanging over the water.

He smiled as he saw Madison line up the kids on the shore, then climbed into the tire swing. The oldest, Suzanne, gave her a hard shove, and as the tire swung out, she leaped and dropped into the water with a rebel yell. She burst through the water, sending the tire back and letting each one climb on for their turn. When it came to Suzanne, she looked toward her father, asking for a push.

Alex instantly set his tea glass down and left the porch, going to Suzanne. He gave her the needed push, and she plunged into the water. From the shore Alex watched Madison as she gave the kids rides on her back, put two in inner tubes and give a six-year-old a swimming lesson. Her smile was infectious, her heart on her sleeve. She loved children, loved getting muddy and playing, and Alex envied her. An only child, he hadn't been around small children since he was a kid.

"Come on in," she called.

He strolled down the dock, closer to where she stood in the water. "No, thanks."

"Chicken." She flicked water at him, and he smiled.

"Don't dare me, woman."

"Why not? You're so hot to talk with Angus you aren't enjoying yourself. When was the last time you had fun?"

He thought about it. "The sailing regatta."

"That was nearly a month ago. I read the papers. And congrats on the win, but you were alone then, huh?"

"It was single man competition." He squatted near her. She watched the kids play, tugging the inner-tube line out to the youngest, Shannon.

"You take that beautiful boat of yours out alone, don't you?"

Most of the women he'd dated weren't around longer than a dinner date. "What are you saying, Madison?"

She glanced at him. "I think you forgot how to have fun."

"Have not."

"Have, too."

Her lips curved devilishly, and if he'd seen it coming, he wouldn't have been so close. She grabbed his shirtfront and yanked. He fell sideways into the water, then quickly came up sputtering, glaring at her.

"Madison, I swear!"

"Not in front of the children."

The others laughed, children clapped.

"Spoilsport." Madison grinned, not the least bit contrite. He'd been on the edge of conversation all day, even responded to that damn cell phone twice.

Angus was getting irritated. And so was she. If he wanted to be with her, then he needed to understand that business conversations weren't on her agenda.

"You're using her—" he nodded to the chubby baby girl in the inner tube "—for protection."

"You don't stand a chance, Yankee. I was raised on the water."

"That makes you what? A mackerel?"

"It's clear that ten years in the South didn't give you our biting repartee."

He yanked off his soggy shoes and socks, giving her a sour look as he tossed them on the dock.

"Relax, Alexander," she said in a low voice, inching closer. "You're going to tick off Angus if you don't accept his hospitality."

He swiped water off his face, watching her come to him. Water lapped at her waist molding the bright aqua-blue suit to her body. "I'm here to seal a deal."

She didn't need the reminder. "But you're trying too hard, and you're the one who asked me to *be with* you. I'm surprised you haven't faxed a conversation to me."

"I'm not that bad, am I?" Real concern laced his tone.

"Yes. You take it all for granted."

He looked affronted. "I remember what it's like not to have any money, be the only kid in school wearing hand-me-downs."

Sympathy shaped her features. "You weren't the only one. You just thought you were." Because that was me, too, she thought.

"That didn't seem to matter at the time." Not when he'd just been released from juvenile hall, Alex thought, and everyone knew it. And was afraid of him.

"But now you have more than most folks, and you still don't enjoy it. Just for this time, will you try?"

Her sincere plea curled through his heart. None of the other women he knew were concerned about his happiness, and he decided to quit comparing her to them. Madison was in a class by herself. "Afraid I'll have a heart attack or something?"

"I bet your blood pressure is over the legal limit."

"If it is, it's nothing to do with work," he said, stripping off the wet polo shirt and tossing it with his shoes.

Madison stared at his wide, muscled chest, her fingers itching to touch the black hair dusting the center. She'd never seen him without a shirt. He was lean and tanned, and her gaze followed the thinning line of hair disappearing into his waistband and the water.

"That look is dangerous, woman."

Her gaze jerked to his. "Nice abs, Yankee." He actually blushed a little.

He slid his arm around her waist, gliding her through the water till she was flush against him. Her hand splayed over his chest, the water offering little barrier between them as he gazed down at her, his free hand on her hip.

"You're starting some funny business."

He ducked, his gaze shifting from her mouth to her eyes. "Uh-huh."

"You make this so hard."

He insinuated his knee between her thighs. "Baby," he growled, "you make me hard."

Energy crackled, the current driving a whimper from her throat. Alex drank it, let it tumble into his mouth as his lips molded hungrily over hers. Her fingers flexed on his chest, and he'd never felt anything so erotic as her touch. He wanted to feel it everywhere, and when her hand rode up his skin, fingers sinking into his hair to press him harder to her mouth, he went willingly. Desire escalated quickly out of control, a brushfire hot and burning, and he crushed her in his arms.

Then suddenly she went lax, sliding under the water, wiggling away, then diving deeper. Alex frowned at the water, searching for her. Panic threaded through him....

Until she jumped on his back, wrapping her arms and legs around him and dragging him down under. They wrestled, and he tickled her.

She popped up, gasping for air. "No, don't! Oh, please stop."

He didn't and she burst with laughter, kicking wildly to get away. But he was stronger, swinging her around to face him, and he lifted her out of the water by her waist.

"My God, Madison, is that a tattoo?" He asked breathlessly, seeing where her suit had hiked up.

She grinned. "Yes. My wild days." She clamped her legs around his waist and lurched back, taking him under with her. Alex dragged her into shallow water.

"Show it to me."

"I don't think so." She adjusted the suit over the body art.

"Come on, darlin', give me a peek."

Exotic heat spiraled up from Madison's knees as he inched closer, winding one arm around her waist.

"Is it a fairy? A butterfly?"

His hand slid to the edge of the suit, fingertips pushing under the fabric. She covered his hand. "No."

"I'm supposed to be your husband. Shouldn't I know these things?"

"Yes. *If* you were my husband."

"She's enchanting, Alex. You're lucky," Angus said, suddenly close.

Through the bank of windows and sliding glass doors, Alex and Angus watched Madison rock the child. It seemed so natural for her, with even a stranger's child, and when the little girl snuggled trustingly against her, jamming her thumb in her mouth, something flexed deep in his chest. She looked so serene. His gaze drifted to Bridgett, her husband behind her, his hands clasped lightly over her belly. And in an instant he imagined Madison like that, and the fantasy of his child growing inside blossomed in his mind.

The thought stunned him. He *had* to keep his objective clear, and he reminded himself that he didn't have the right to even think those thoughts. This was a business arrangement. She didn't trust him. She didn't like the man he was, only tolerated him. They didn't have the same goals and future in mind. She felt sorry for him. That's why she was here, why she was being so nice. So charming. So damned sexy.

Alex forced a smile. He wasn't lucky. She wasn't his. Just borrowed. And even if he wanted her after this week, he understood Madison Holt was the "marry and spend a lifetime loving" kind of woman. And his track record stunk worse than the Savannah river at low tide. Enough to know he didn't have what it took to get a relationship right. Silently he insisted he liked his life the way it was—safe. No complications. But just the same, he studied her, gold light showering over her and the dark-haired baby. She looked up, meeting his gaze through the glass. Alex felt hit between the eyes for just a second. He didn't know by what, but it almost hurt to look at her.

"God, she is so incredibly beautiful," he whispered, unaware he'd spoken aloud.

Angus and his sons-in-law chuckled, and Alex glanced sheepishly, then quietly slid the glass door open.

"Hi." Madison rubbed the baby's back in slow circles.

He closed the door behind him for privacy, leaning against the porch post. "Hard to believe that was the same child running hell-bent through this house a half hour ago."

She pressed her lips to a pile of brown curls. "She's just learned to walk. My nephew is like that, a spinning top one second, then out cold the next."

"Nephew?"

"My younger sister's son." At his surprised look, she added, "I have three brothers and a sister. I'm the oldest."

No wonder she was so comfortable around this crowd. Even before his parents died, he'd felt he was missing out on something.

Randy slipped out, smiling first at Alex, then Madison. "Ah-h, Her Highness sleeps," he said, taking the child. "Thanks, Madison. You've got the touch."

"She's beautiful, Randy."

"She makes me feel so insignificant. Amazing, huh?" He smiled with pride, nuzzling his daughter's neck. "What is it about babies' skin that's so... comforting?" He stepped back inside, and the little family headed to the bedrooms full of children.

Madison sighed, watching them go, then looked at her hands.

"You want one, don't you?"

"A few years ago that was the furthest thing from my mind. And yes, someday, I want many."

"What changed your mind?"

"My mom died when I was fifteen and I had to step in, fill her shoes. I practically raised my brothers and sister, and when I had the chance, I ran as fast as I could away from that life. I tried everything in my power to obliterate by it moving to New York." She looked into the house as if she could see through the walls. "But I always wanted to come home, always felt better about myself when I did. The harder I fought who I really was, the more unhappy I was."

"And who are you now?"

She met his gaze and shrugged. "More country than city, I suppose. Not that being citified doesn't have its benefits," she said, giving him the once-over. "It's just not my style." She stood, gazing out at the dark velvet lake, looking forlorn.

He remembered what pushed her to leave; carving up a company rooted in her hometown. What had she said? *I'd forgotten what's important.* Family.

Until he'd been here, seen her with the kids, the O'Malleys, Alex had forgotten what it was like to be around a family, be around a woman like her. He'd always steered clear of her kind. He wondered if she had any prospects to fulfil her plans. In the back of his mind, Alex wanted to be the one to make her happy, fill her dreams.

Fantasy.

This was temporary. His future hung on one word from Angus. She didn't believe he could handle something stronger than this play they enacted. That stung, he admitted, but he'd given her no reason to believe otherwise. Heck, he'd never had reason to believe it himself.

Yet Madison was intoxicating as warm brandy.

And he was addicted, he thought, turning her toward him, pressing his lips to her temple.

She met his gaze, her brows drawn slightly. "You okay?"

He nodded, a turmoil of feelings running through him.

"Come on, let's say good-night." Moving out of his arms, she clasped his hand, pulling him after her. "It's time to go home."

Smiling to himself, Alex followed obediently. Home. Damn, that sounded good.

They went in separate directions when they entered the room. Madison tried to ignore him, the intimacy of him rifling for his clothes in the drawers beside her, the way he sat in the chair and removed his shoes, placing them neatly in the closet. She kicked hers in and decided to be out of the bathroom before he was out of the one on the opposite side of the suite.

When Alex came out of the bathroom he was alone, then noticed the breeze coming from the open deck doors. He crossed to them, stilling for a second when he saw her lying in the chaise, her silk robe exposing her legs to the tops of her thighs.

"Damn, Madison."

She gasped and covered herself to her throat. "I

thought you were still in the shower." He was bare-chested, wearing only cotton, drawstring slacks and looking too damn masculine for her tastes right now.

"If you thought to drive me nuts, being naked under that is doing it."

"I'm not naked." She gave him a quick peek at her chemise strap.

"Close enough." He grasped her ankles, lifting them before sitting at the foot of her chaise.

"There is room over there." She gestured to the matching chair.

"The view is better here." He nestled her feet on his lap, rubbing the sole of one foot.

"Oh, you're hired," she moaned, closing her eyes as he plied strong fingers to her sore feet.

"Those rocks in the lake hurt, I bet."

"I didn't notice it until now."

"Okay, confess, when and where did you get that tattoo?"

She smiled, laughing to herself and shaking her head. "In college. It was like a pact, one perpetrated by lots of Bahama Mama cocktails, mind you, and made at a sorority party night. A group of us got them."

"Katherine, too?"

"Oh, yes."

The mystery of it was driving him crazy. "Now that's hard to believe, Kat of all people. She's so sophisticated."

She cocked her head. "Should I be insulted?"

"Of course not."

"Good, I didn't want to have to knock your teeth in."

He grinned, massaging up her calf. "Thanks for today."

"I had a good time. They're nice people." Closing her eyes, she moaned as his fingers ground into her knotted calf. "I'll think I'll keep you around just to rub my feet."

"I'll rub anything you want."

Her eyes flew open. Before she could say anything, he yanked on her feet, dragging her closer. For a split second he stared before he kissed her. And the heat lingering beneath the surface burst to flame, splintering through her, and she squeezed his biceps, holding on as his mouth moved roughly over hers. She opened for him, then moaned as his tongue plunged inside. So good, she thought, so right.

He kissed her and kissed her, drawing her onto his lap.

Her fingers drove into his hair, dribbled down his throat to his chest. She molded and shaped him as his hands found their way beneath her satin robe.

It was raw, he thought, this hunger, igniting with the merest touch, driving him crazy with the sensations he experienced by just hearing her little whimpers of pleasure. But the feel of her skin was an incredible aphrodisiac. She was soft and scented, so feminine, and that wildness, like a mountain cat, lingered just beneath the surface. He could feel it in her, taste it in her kiss, in the pressure of her breasts against his chest.

In the way her fingers played daringly over him.

"You feel so good, Maddy."

Madison drew back, her arms on his shoulders as she forced her breathing to slow down. Mercy. She was ready to explode, and it wouldn't take much more to give up her resolve and indulge.

"Are you trying to seduce me?" she breathed against his mouth.

He kissed her briefly, a wet slide that made her gasp. "I was going to ask you the same thing."

"Then I guess we'd better stop this."

"Are you always so level-headed?"

"Not when you kiss me."

He smiled. "Nice to know I can weaken you a little."

She arched a brow.

"You can't believe for a second I'm not coming apart at the seams every time we touch."

Yes, she did believe it, because sensations were still rocketing through her body and testing her courage. She wanted him as she had wanted no other man. He was a sexy, desirable playboy. But she was merely convenient. "All the more reason to say good-night now, Alexander." She left his lap.

Alex watched her vanish into the suite, then braced his elbows on his knees and clutched his head in his hands. He drew a shaky breath. His body throbbed like a tribal drum, the tempo slow to ease.

He shouldn't have laid a hand on her, but her wild streak lured and he was a sucker for it. He was heading for trouble if he gave in to temptation again. No, he thought, looking up and watching her slip beneath the sheets. It was already here.

He hadn't touched her since last night. Not a casual brush, not a single kiss. Not even for Angus's benefit. Madison almost wished he'd touch her. Anything would be better than the incredible tension running along with her blood. She knew he was trying to ignore her, put distance between them, yet he was the kind of man women sensed before seeing, his every look was filled with a heated message. So much that Angus asked if there was something wrong just as they'd left. She felt isolated, greedy for his touch even when she reminded herself that any more than kisses and a couple spine-wracking touches—she'd be deep in the mud, sucked into him like quicksand. Fighting the pull was harder than breathing and she felt like a high-strung racehorse, chomping to be free.

During the ride back to the inn and the trip in the elevator, unnamed sensations simmered, making her skin tingle, her senses acute to the man beside her. It was as if she could feel his body beneath his clothes, the sheer sensuality of him. It taunted her, and his dark glances, smoldering and aware, scraped her like claws.

One dig and she'd peel down to her skin for him.

He pushed open the hotel room door, the fragrance of warm apples and cinnamon breezing the air as he flipped on a lamp. She followed him in. He crossed the room to the ice bucket and popped the cork of a bottle of Chardonnay. He glanced at her, his look inquiring and she shook her head and with a bundle of her clothes, slipped into the bathroom. Her shower only served to sharpen her body's awareness, of him and her own feelings, and when she stepped out of the bathroom, he was near the living room, his gaze moving heavily over her.

Savage. Electrifying.

Alex felt like a stag scenting his doe, the space between them feeling like inches instead of yards. Behind him the huge bed loomed, the air fragrant with hot spice and cloaked in darkness. He watched her move to the dresser and put her things away, the long maroon satin robe shifting over her skin like liquid. Part of him wondered if she was naked beneath it. Part of him wished she was bound to her throat like a nun.

She never looked more elusive to him than she did now.

Every nuance was wrapped in a catlike sensuality and he told himself that was her lure—the dark fire brewing in her—but he knew otherwise. It was her. The woman who drew lines around herself as he had around his own world; the woman who held a stranger's baby as if it were her own and made heads turn when she walked into a room. A woman who forced him to step back and look at his life and see its value against the simplest of things.

She came toward him, the satin molding her incredible legs parting enough to show their sleek-muscled lines and making him crave to touch and taste every inch of her. The day-long denial made him reach when he shouldn't, his fingers brushing her arm. She stilled, her gaze colliding with his. Her eyes were glossy, on the verge of tears.

Something hard shattered inside him.

He whispered her name, his hand sliding over her stomach, fingers curling around her waist, and when he urged, she came to him, plowing her fingers into his hair and tipping his head to hers.

The first touch of her mouth was soft, like a breeze, and when her tongue slid over the line of his lips, Alex came apart, claiming her mouth with the ferocity he'd held in check. Hot. Possessive. And she stole a piece of him with every touch of her lips, with every part of herself she gave him so willingly.

Each shift and moan ground through him, weakening him, softening his knees. His hands rode up her back, pushing her tighter to his chest.

Madison gripped his hair and ravaged his mouth and knew she could put a stop to this with one word. But that would take thinking—and she only wanted to feel. And when his hands swept her body, parting the robe, shaping her ribs, then enfolding her breasts, she let him, purring for him as he rubbed, toyed with her nipples through the silk chemise. Her kiss grew stronger, hotter, her hands skipping over his shoulders, feeling his strength.

He staggered back, sinking into the love seat and shifting her to straddle his lap, tasting the slender line of her throat, pushing the robe off her shoulders to pool and catch at her elbows. She rose up, offering, and he tugged the chemise straps down. Cool, spiced air hit her bare breasts.

"Beautiful," he murmured as he wrapped his lips around her nipple, drawing deeply.

She gasped and arched, whispering his name and clutching him to her breasts as he tasted and played, his teeth scoring the tender underside before he dragged his tongue around her nipples again and again. Her breath shuddered, her sex hot against his stomach, and he opened his eyes, meeting her gaze.

She licked her lips, watching his tongue move over her flesh as if she were sweet cream for the taking. She couldn't pull her gaze away. It was too erotic to ignore, felt too good to stop, and when his hands found their way beneath the satin, enfolding her buttocks, she groaned at the splendid feeling of his palms on her naked flesh. She was alive now, feminine and desired. Hungry for pleasure. Now.

"Your skin is so smooth." He squeezed and pushed her down against him, his arousal separated from her by only slivers of cloth. She whispered his name, thrusting subtly against him, taking his mouth with a wildness that defied thought. His fingers dipped into her dewy folds, and she whimpered against his lips, clawing, rocking.

"You're on the edge, aren't you?"

She nodded shakily.

"Let me see it." His hand slipped deeper between them, fingers parting her and she flexed, gripping his shoulders. He stroked her delicately and she gasped for breath, over and over.

"Alexander!"

"You're almost there. Do you know what that does to me?"

She thrust against his arousal. "I have an idea."

He smiled, wrapping one arm around her waist, pressing her tight to his groin even as he pushed two fingers inside her.

Eyes locked and held. Alex plied her rhythmically, loving her darkening eyes, her soft, panting breaths. Loving that she was as bold and wild as he'd imagined and that she let him give her this—see this. She rocked and he pushed, aching to be inside her, feel her wrap and grab him. She covered his hand, flinching, riding. Alex watched her climax, felt it quiver, ripping through her and into him. He kissed her, devouring her cries, and he held her as her body clenched with a near violent explosion. Alex trembled with the power of it, felt her quaking slowly fade until she let out a soft shudder and she sank against him, burying her face in his shoulder.

"What a magnificent thing to see." She made a pained sound. He rubbed her back, pulling the chemise straps up, then tipping her head till she met his gaze. His gaze searched hers. "You have nothing to be ashamed of. Nothing."

"I'm not." She tried leaving his lap, but he held her. "I'm embarrassed."

"Aw, baby, don't be. Please." He brushed his mouth lightly over hers, loving her instant response. "I liked giving you pleasure as much as seeing it." His voice lowered to a dusky pitch. "But the next time, I want to taste that explosion."

She moaned and reddened, pressing her forehead to his. "You just want to see my tattoo."

Only then did he realize he hadn't.

"You gotta let me see." His hand slid beneath her robe and under her chemise.

His touch felt undeniably arousing, yet Madison shook her head, then kissed him softly, loving how his arms slowly wrapped her, squeezed her. Her embarrassment faded to comfort, the intimacy shared crossing another invisible line both tried to avoid. She drew back, her fingertips lingering over his handsome face as the impact of his unselfishness bloomed through her. She slid from his lap and crossed to the deck doors, staring at the glittering black lake, folding her arms over her middle and bracing her shoulder on the frame.

Alex frowned at the solemn look on her face, the way she hugged herself as if she needed protection from him. He wanted her so badly he could taste desire, feel it running through his veins at a hard charge, yet her expression spoke more than she was saying. She was scared. Of him. Of being a fictitious notch on his bedpost, of being discarded. He never expected her to accommodate him after that little bit of pleasure, yet he couldn't predict the future. His own was dangling in the air right now. But it was her forlorn expression that made him feel helpless—and responsible. The last thing he wanted to do was to hurt this woman.

Madison sensed him move up behind her, felt the warmth of his body against her, and without pause she leaned into him, laying her head back on his shoulder. His arms wrapped around her, and he buried his face in the curve of her throat, inhaling, his hand smoothing over her stomach, her ribs. Her muscles flexed with new desire, and she reached up, plowing her fingers into his hair.

"You okay?" he asked.

She nodded, unable to voice her confused feelings past the sudden knot in her throat. She reminded herself not to read anything into this intimacy beyond consenting adults having a little fun. Believing every man she dated was the Mr. Right of her life was a ridiculous fantasy. And as wonderful as those moments in his arms were, Alex was certainly no exception to the rule. But the hard truth was that her feelings for him refused to follow the rules.

"Talk to me. What did I do?"

The hurt in his voice felt like a fresh wound. "Nothing, Alexander. It's nothing you've done."

"Well, something's got you down." His lips brushed her ear as he added, "I was hoping I'd put a smile on your face. Was I wrong?"

"No, oh, no." She turned in his arms. "That was wonderful."

His hands on her stilled for a second, his gaze searching hers. "Is that so bad?"

"Yes, when this is temporary, and we are worlds apart."

"No expectations, isn't that what you said?"

She felt duly warned. "Good night, Alexander." She left him, moving to the far side of the bed and sliding beneath the sheets. She didn't look back, lost in her thoughts.

Alex stared at her huddled form for a long moment, hating that she was hurting, when only moments ago she was panting with pleasure, and realizing he was the reason for both. He didn't like feeling like this. It was unfamiliar—but he didn't want to fight it so hard anymore, either.

# Eight

**M**adison wouldn't tell him. She couldn't. Every man she'd been intimate with always went running the instant they knew she was a virgin. Men wanted their women pure as a fairy-tale princess, but none were prepared to make love to a virgin. Maybe they'd feel obligated to her, or threatened by "being the first." Perhaps there were women who'd get some notion about love and forever. Madison didn't. Her sister's situation, unmarried with a child, was proof enough of that misunderstanding. Yet experience told her it was the quickest way to douse runaway passion. Men, she knew, didn't want to be held accountable for making that first experience memorable since it would hurt. Ironic, she thought, for the responsibility was hers, not theirs, and she'd decided after her last relationship that if she really wanted to give up her virtue, she'd never reveal the truth until it was too late.

She looked at Alex asleep on the far side of the bed. She had no expectations and couldn't allow a future to materialize, not in her mind or her heart. Her happiness didn't hinge on a man. Alexander Donahue was a confirmed bachelor, despite the feelings they shared. When this ''marriage'' was over, he would run from her. She knew it. She wouldn't expect any more.

''Why so sad?''

She inhaled, startled and rolled to her side, clutching the sheet to her breasts. ''Good morning. I thought you were asleep.''

Alex scoffed, not liking her evasiveness. ''With you this close?''

His compliment made Madison feel incredibly sexy. ''Hungry? I could order up some breakfast.''

''I have a better solution.'' On top of the sheets, his hand slid across the bed, gliding over her stomach.

''Alexander,'' she warned, yet didn't stop him, couldn't stop him.

He pulled her to him. ''I love it when you say my name. Makes me feel like I'm the only man in the world with it and you're the only one who can say it.''

Her eyes burned, and she brushed inky-black hair from his forehead, loving that he briefly closed his eyes.

''How about a kiss?''

''You're like that commercial. You can't have just one.''

''Not when they taste so damn good.''

''You're not playing fair.''

He loomed over her, his expression serious. "Who said I was playing?"

She stilled, gazing up at him, refusing to read anything into that. "I thought you were going to show me how good you were at sailing this morning?"

His mouth rolled softly over hers. "In a minute."

She worried his lips with her own, and he shifted closer, his groin pressing to hers through the covers. He hardened against her, and she ached to touch him, know him, yet when her hand rested on his hip, he suddenly drew back, gazing into her eyes for an instant before he flopped back onto the bed.

"Alex?"

"Go, get ready," he said to the ceiling. "Hurry. 'Cause more than the tide is up."

She laughed lightly, slipping from the bed, and Alex forced himself not to watch her walk to the closet for her clothes. He didn't need any more temptation. Her perfume alone drove him nuts. She needed to trust him, was just beginning to, and he wasn't going to blow this relationship because she was the hottest creature he'd ever touched. He wanted more of Madison Holt than her body.

Madison cast the fishing line, her legs adjusting to the rocking of the boat as Alex lowered the anchor, watching her. She set the rod in the harness and stepped down from the edge. He patted the space beside him, and his heart tripped when she sank against him.

"I didn't know you liked to fish."

"Love it. What could be better than lounging around waiting for the food to come to you?" She tipped her head to look at him. "I throw a mean shrimp net, too."

He smiled, studying her face. "All those secrets."

"I don't hide anything from you, Alexander. Which is more than I can say for you."

Emotion drained from his features like an emptying glass. "I don't want to talk about the past."

"She hurt you that bad?"

He looked away, squinting in the sun.

"You owe me that."

"I don't owe you anything."

She felt the chill in the air as if winter had settled. She left the bench, but he lurched after her, grasping her shoulder. She twisted.

The gloss in her eyes clawed him right there and then. "Aw, Madison."

"I didn't hurt you, Alexander." Her lips trembled. "Don't make me pay for it."

"I'm sorry. Come back and sit with me."

A look of indecision crept over her beautiful face.

"Please."

The little word wilted her intentions.

Sitting side by side, he coiled nylon rope, the sails snapping against the wind and rocking the craft. He stared out at the boats littering the water like stars on a dark blue sky and it was a long moment before he spoke. When he did, his voice was lifeless, dead.

"Her name was Celeste. We were together for a year. I adored her. She wanted to be my wife."

That he could admit to adoring any woman sent a streak of jealousy through her. "Sounds fine so far."

He shook his head, pain rippling over his features before they cooled to a dark mask. "No. She wanted

to be the wife of Donahue Enterprises' president."
He looked at her then. "Not mine."

"Ah, she liked the life-style more." She flipped
open the cooler and took out two sodas, offering him
one.

"She claimed she wanted a home."

"Did you want that, too?" She popped the top and
sipped.

He shrugged, rolling the can between his palms.
"When I have to travel to make deals and worry
about becoming obsolete with technology or whether
or not I'm going to make the payroll, yeah, sometimes."

Sometimes wasn't enough in her book. A person
wasn't a sometimes husband or a sometimes wife.
And a home wasn't where you slept, in her opinion—
it was where you lived and raised a family. Alex just
didn't get it, and she was suddenly thankful she'd left
New York before she got caught up in the power
climb and forgot it herself. "Having money isn't all
it's cracked up to be, is it?"

He made a rude sound. "Has a tendency to cloud
the thinking. I wish I'd seen it before it went that
far."

"Was she 'wife material'?"

"In the beginning, I suppose." *But not like you*,
Alex thought, meeting her gaze. *Nothing like you.*

"Those seem like regular problems, Alex. Things
you have to work out between husband and wife.
Maybe you gave up too easily?"

"Maybe. She did. I was just getting out of the red
and before I bought up the cell air, there were months
when I didn't think I'd make it and that I would let
everyone down. I came back early from a meeting

and found her in bed, my bed, with one of the executives I was negotiating with for the cells.'' He remembered the humiliation. ''Worst thing was, everyone knew it, knew she was giving details of the deals while searching for richer ground. I was too busy trying to make it all work to see the signs.''

''She couldn't have loved you, Alex. Not and betray you so easily.''

''I know. Maybe I didn't love her as much as I thought, either.''

''There's your trouble.'' She braced her back on the wooden bench, sipping the soda. ''Love is supposed to be feeling, not thinking. If you have to think that hard, then you aren't there.''

That sounded too simple, he thought. ''You speaking from experience?''

''Not as much as you, I imagine.'' She tore her gaze from his, a little sting flitting through her chest with the memory. Paul had wanted everything from her; time, attention, and before she'd made the mistake and given him her body, she'd realized he gave her nothing.

''Who was he?''

She glanced. ''A man who couldn't understand my wants and didn't have the time or the inclination to find them out.'' Which was the case with most of the men she'd dated. Her family's welfare came first right now. She was raised that way, and she didn't mind being a rock for them. The trouble was that men didn't like that she took care of her obligations first, before them.

Yet for Alex she'd ignored everything. She'd packed hastily, called her sister and father to tell them she wouldn't be around and that there were plenty of meals in the freezer. Only Katherine knew where she was. She'd discarded everything for him, and that scared her.

"She wasn't the first woman to split for richer territory."

Oh, to have so many women turn on him, she thought. "Sounds like the wrong choices were yours."

"I have a string of those, believe me."

She frowned.

On the bench, he turned toward her, staring at her as he spoke. "After my parents died, I went wild. I was mad at Mom for getting cancer, at Dad for dying of a broken heart and leaving me alone. Got myself thrown out of a dozen foster homes until I ended up in jail."

Her eyes widened a bit. "Jail?"

"Yeah, talk about scaring a kid silly. It was petty stuff—vandalism and disturbing the peace. My father's lawyer found me somehow and asked me what my parents would say if they saw me. I was ashamed, and that terrified me more than prison. I knew I had to straighten myself out or end up on the streets." He shrugged. "I figured the only way I could make it right was to get back the company like Dad wanted."

Madison still thought it was too much to ask of a young boy, but kept her comments to herself. "You will."

"I have to. It's as if I can't live until I get it."

She heard the frustration in his voice. "I understand. Sometimes I feel as if I've put my life on hold for my family. Don't get me wrong, I want to take care of them, but I wish I didn't have to. That sounds selfish, I suppose."

"Not to me. It's something you have to do right now."

She smiled. "How far you've come, Alexander," she marveled. "It's amazing. More so that you did it alone. I'm impressed as hell."

His heart, he swore, swelled and shot to the sun. "Thanks, Maddy. That means a lot to me."

"How much?" She puckered her lips like a fish.

"Much." Smiling, he slid his hand behind her neck, tipping her head to lay his mouth over hers in a slow kiss. Wind buffeted them, tearing her hair loose and spreading it across his face like spilled silk. He tried for calm, for patience, when he wanted to crush her to him and feel every lush inch of her against him.

"More," she muttered against his lips, inching closer. "I can feel your restraint. Don't hide how you feel. Not from me, please."

In a heartbeat, he dragged her onto his lap, and she curled around him, her arms around his neck and her fingers in his hair. She devoured him, aching so deeply in her belly for him—for the boy he'd been, the man he'd become and the lover he wanted to be. She'd never met a man who tried so hard to not want her or who kissed like madness and made her wish she'd dumped her virtue years before. Especially when he ran his hands over her hips and down her legs as if she'd disappear. She worked her hands under his shirt, rubbing his chest, her thumbs rasping over his nipples before diving lower.

He groaned, deepening his kiss and was laying her back on the bench when the reel snapped, then spun rapidly. She broke the kiss, smiling at his disappointment. "Here, fishy, fishy." She kissed him once more, hard and quick, then scrambled off his lap to stop the line. Reeling the line in, she glanced back. He was rubbing his thighs and breathing hard. His arousal tented his khaki shorts.

"Damn, Madison."

She felt exotic and powerful. "My, my. What a nice compliment." He threw her a dark look. "It's the justice of nature that women don't have so obvious a sign."

"Oh, yeah?" His gaze lowered meaningfully to her breasts, her nipples thrusting against the navy T-shirt.

"Cold air."

"It's eighty degrees out," he countered wryly, loving her sly smile.

The rod jerked, and she focused on the fish, calling, "Come to Mama, fishy."

Alex watched her fight the biggest fish he'd ever seen, laughing as it nearly snapped the rod, then catching her around the waist when it almost took her into the water to avoid capture. Her excitement was his, and he made a big deal of it, taking her picture with it on the bow of the sailboat. The fish wiggled on the hook, its tail slapping her shoulder, and she suddenly rushed to the rail and released it, shouting, "Be free, escape!" before falling into his arms, laughing wildly.

Fish stink and all, Alex swore it was the best time he'd ever had.

The instant they stepped into the suite the phone rang.

"Angus. We were just changing to—oh, no kidding." Alex covered the phone. "Bridgett went into labor this morning. He's calling from the hospital."

She smiled. ''Does Randy need help with Shannon?''

Alex relayed the message, thinking how easily she offered her help. He shook his head at her, then gave Angus his cell phone number and asked if he'd call with the news. Angus assured him this wouldn't delay the renewal of his and Laura's vows on Saturday.

He hung up, slipping around the door of the bathroom, watching her wash her face and brush the tangles from her hair. ''Wanna do something? We're free for a while.''

''Like what?''

His smoldering gaze roamed her from head to toe. ''I could think of one or two things, and we wouldn't have to leave the room.''

A sweet tingling skipped through her body, and her gaze clashed with his in the mirror. ''Behave.''

He grinned, utterly fascinated as she freshened her lipstick.

''There's a festival this afternoon and street dance tonight.''

''Great,'' he said. ''Let's go.''

''Let me change first.''

He looked down at her white shorts and navy T-shirt as she left the bathroom. ''Madison. You look fine.''

''Ick, no. I'm wearing fish slime.'' She flicked through clothes hanging in the closet. He folded his arms over his chest and frowned, impatient. ''It's a girl thing, deal with it,'' she said, closing the bathroom door in his face.

The rewards of living with her, he thought, was seeing her as she really was. While dating, people put their best foot forward, often artificial, but Madison didn't disguise a thing. She'd rather be outside than in, dine from a vendor's cart than in a restaurant. She wanted to make the bed, though housekeeping would, yet misplaced things constantly, raking through her drawers and bags in search of the elusive item. She tossed her shoes in the closet in a pile while his were in neat rows.

And when she left the bathroom, wearing a short, deep fuchsia tank dress and matching sandals, looking as if she'd walked off the cover of a magazine, Alex decided it was worth the wait. Even with the extra five minutes while she searched for her purse.

"You aren't going to shop, are you?"

He sounded like a kid asking if he had to get a shot, she thought, grabbing his hand and dragging him to the door. "Sure. Maybe we'll find something for Bridgett."

"Bridgett? Not the baby?"

She glanced back. "Of course, but to the best of my knowledge, it's the mother who does all the work, and while everyone is oohing and ahhing over the newborn and congratulating the father, she needs to feel some of the attention. Keeps back the postpartum blues."

He was considering that when they stepped off the elevator. "Maybe something for Shannon, then, too? She might feel jealous." Stopping short, she met his gaze, her tender smile sinking like arrows into his heart.

"Oh, Alexander." Her fingertips whispered over his cheek. "I knew there was a warm, considerate man in there somewhere."

He slid his arm around her waist and whispered, "I thought that's what I was last night."

She ducked her head. "Stop teasing me about that."

Pulling her close, he pressed his lips near her ear and growled, "I can't help it. I keep seeing you, hearing you, *feeling* you. You pulse. Did you know that?" Madison gripped his shirtfront, her body throbbing to life, and she lifted her gaze. "And you make me feel as if I'm worthy of touching someone like you."

His uncertainty stole her breath, her heart, and Madison went up on her toes and kissed him. "You are, Alexander, or I wouldn't have let this go that far."

His throat tightened and he swallowed, wondering how he could feel pleased and scared at the same time.

He won a stuffed rabbit for her by pitching rings on bottlenecks, and she rewarded him with a wet, sloppy kiss that made him want to win the world for her. Then she upstaged him, shooting at wooden ducks, and won an honest-to-goodness rawhide wallet, complete with loop stitching. She had his initials burned into it, then insisted he must use it. Alex smiled every time he took it out to pay for another load of junk food.

He forgot everything around her; the line they drew between each other, the toy company, the lies they perpetrated. Before nightfall Angus called on the cellular to say it was a false alarm and Bridgett was home. Alex begged off for the night, and Angus simply chuckled and said he understood. Alex felt remorse for the lie hanging over them like a boom about to drop, but when Madison pulled him into the street dance, getting wild with the crowd, he dismissed his concern as he watched her wiggle and shake to the music.

They made out like teenagers on the Ferris wheel, then sat on the rocks near the water, talking till the sun turned red-gold. He laughed at her jokes, loved touching her and that she touched him. Something inside him came apart every time she did.

On the ride up in the elevator, he gathered her in his arms. "You're about the best time I've ever had, Madison."

She smiled, her eyes suspiciously bright. "Low threshold of excitement, huh?"

"Not anymore," he said, brushing her hair off her face and watching the motion. She enjoyed life, although he suspected she worked harder than she let on. He was tempted to call Katherine and bug her for details, but decided he wanted to discover them himself. And in that moment Alex realized just how much she meant to him. And in such a short time.

"Want dinner?"

"After all the junk food? No, thanks. How about a movie and maybe room service later?" She stepped into the room.

"You sure?"

"I want to shower and then be a slug. A real couch potato. You game?"

He closed them inside. "Yeah, I'm game." He backed her up against the door, and she wound her arms around him. "But you know what lying on a couch with you will do to me."

"I'm sure you can control yourself."

His hand swept low on her spine, pulling her into him. "But can you?"

She laughed and blushed, and he kissed her, a deep

push into her mouth, into her body. His kiss grew harder, hungrier, and when her fingertips slid over the waist of his trousers, then brushed across the front, Alex thought he'd explode right there.

"I need to shower," she said, pulling away as she slipped into the bathroom.

She could feel him on the other side, hear him mutter to himself before he walked away. She quickly stripped and stepped into a hot shower. She shampooed her hair and washed, the strong pricking streams of water beating against her breasts, heightening the sensitivity of her skin. Madison wished he would join her in the shower now. The thought of it nearly drove her mad with desire, and she left the shower, slipping into the complementary terry-cloth robe and toweling her hair dry.

"Madison," he said softly from the other side of the door.

"Yes."

His hands braced on the door frame, Alex pressed his forehead to the wood. "Let me in."

"Why?"

"Because I need to see you. Touch you. I'm going mad with it."

Her heart skipped. "Alex—"

"Hush. Listen to me. Just listen." There was a long hesitation before he said, "I want to make love with you, but not because you and I are here together, alone. Even if you were on the other side of the world, I would feel the same. We have something good going...and you know it."

Madison closed her eyes.

"No matter what my reputation says or what you've thought of me in the past, you know we're good together. Hell, darlin', we're great. I can't guarantee where it will lead or if it will last, but—"

The door coasted open.

His arms raised, hands on the frame still, they stared.

"Nobody can guarantee how they'll feel, Alexander. Or for how long."

His features tightened, his gaze hot with his emotions. "I want you in my life, Madison. You're under my skin...." He swallowed hard, lowering his arms and stepping inside. "And I want you to stay."

Madison choked, aware what that cost him, a man like him, a man without love in his life for so long. A man who didn't trust himself. She slid her arms around his neck, her fingers sinking into his inky-black hair. "Oh, Alex, we really shouldn't be doing this."

"Yes, we should." His mouth covered hers, a kiss deep with want and longing. "But say you don't want this and I'll go sleep in the car. Hell, I'll go beg Angus for a spot on his couch." He gripped her shoulders, staring into her eyes. "Tell me, and I'll behave and never touch you again and just go mad in a corner like the depraved creature that I am."

She swore she fell in love with him right then. "I don't want you to go." Her hands slid down his bare chest to his waistband. "And I certainly don't want you to behave." She tugged the strings. "Because I won't."

With a sultry smile, she dipped her hand inside.

# Nine

Alex caught her hand, then caught her to him, crushing her mouth beneath his own, his tongue darting and sweeping and making her moan in a way that drove him crazy. Just the thought that she wanted him, wanted to pleasure him, delivered him to the depths of his need. Passion fractured, unleashed and ripping through them. All the subtle touches, the looks and stolen kisses culminating in a flash fire of greed and hunger and a need neither could ignore.

Alex tried for patience, but when her nails raked lightly over his nipples, the strength of his kiss drove her back. Her bottom hit the counter. He lifted her onto it, his hips spreading her thighs, his mouth greedily trailing down her throat. He parted the robe, baring her breasts, cupping them before he bent. His lips closed over one tight peak and she whimpered, offering herself in wild abandon.

This, she thought, trying to catch her breath, was divine madness. He laved, his teeth scoring the soft underside before he took a second plump nipple into the heat of his mouth again and again…and leaving her mindless with sensations.

"Alex, we…oh, yeeesss," she gasped, licking her lips. "We…we need protection."

He straightened, capturing her mouth, refusing to pause even for an instant as he reached blindly for his shaving kit, overturning the contents into the sink. He rummaged, then crushed packets into her palm.

She tore her mouth from his and blinked. "That's quite a few."

"We'll need them." He pulled her off the counter, back stepping, sprinkling hot grinding kisses over her throat and bare shoulders.

The bed only inches away, he paused in the center of the living room, needing the feel of her flesh next to his, soft yielding to hard. Her lips swept the curve of his ear, and he shuddered. Her hand dipped deep inside his slacks, fingers closing around his arousal. He threw his head back and groaned like a beast suddenly set free.

"Madison," he moaned, his knees going soft. Nothing in his life felt better than her touch.

He trembled for her, and Madison felt empowered, a boldness rising in her as she watched pleasure float over his features. She wasn't innocent. She'd seen enough, done enough to be prepared. And she was eager to feel him, to be filled and stroked and loved. By him. Only him. She hungered more than she ever thought possible, and her aching body begged to lose herself in him, the years of suppression rising to the surface. She had never been more ready in her life.

"You're so warm," she whispered. "And you throb for me." Her gaze never wavered as she slid her fingers over the smooth tip of him.

He flattened her hand on him, then drew it to his chest. "You keep doing that and I'll do more than throb," he said into her mouth, then kissed her, drawing her to the bed. Fishing in her robe pocket, he tossed the packets on the bed, nipping her smooth, flawless shoulder.

"Show me."

She held his gaze, untying her sash, parting her robe.

His smoldering gaze raked down to her bare toes and back up. "I knew you were gorgeous." He looked again, pushing the robe down her arms to pool on the floor. "I just didn't imagine this."

Madison felt proud and beautiful as he swept her hair back and kissed her, a never-ending layer of his lips and tongue over her body. He had an amazing mouth. And he knew how to use it. He worshiped her breasts, her ribs, her stomach, and her fingertips dug into his shoulders, knees liquefying as he tasted the dip of her waist, her navel, the sweep of her hip with exquisite care.

"Nor this." He laved his tongue over the tiniest tattoo, chuckling to himself.

"You'd do anything to see that."

"Oh, yes." Gently, he pushed her onto the bed, hovering over her long enough to lick her a path to her dark brown curls between her thighs.

"Alex?"

"I crave you like candy." He nipped the inside of her thigh. "And I want to taste it." He spread her, his tongue immediately delving.

She cried out and arched, calling his name in a long, breathy moan, writhing elegantly, and if Alex had thought long enough, he'd swear she'd never experienced anything like it.

Madison hadn't. Never. Ever. And any thought of denying herself flew from her mind. She lost herself beneath his touch, his expertise sweeping her quickly to the brink of rapture. He pushed her knees up, draping them over his shoulders, driving deeper, then thrust two fingers inside her.

Her body fractured, clenched and she begged him to stop. On a dastardly chuckle, he refused, loving her quaking, her cries and moans and the little jerks of her body as she rode his mouth helplessly to the end of pleasure. A little sob caught in her throat as she sank into the bed.

She panted, swiping the hair off her face as he moved onto the bed beside her. Flinging a leg over his hip, she slid her hand inside his slacks.

"Don't. Stop. Oh, no," he said deadpan as he ducked, worrying the tip of her breast, feeling her nipple peak on his tongue.

She freed him into her palm. "Oh, Alex, is that for me?" she said inside a devious laugh.

"Always."

She stroked him. Not that Alex needed any more stimulation. Just watching her undress him, curl away to tug his slacks free, which she was most eager to do, left him quaking with desire. He ground down on his control, the urge to push her on her back and be inside her scraping him raw. She crawled up him, over his legs, smiling, soft and mysterious, before she slicked her tongue over the tip of him. His muscles seized, and he dragged her up and kissed her with the ferocity of a man gone wild.

His lungs worked. "I want you all night long." He said it like a complaint.

"But I want you now." She pushed him to his back, then straddled him.

He arched a brow, his hands smoothing over her buttocks and thighs. He was shaking, badly, like a boy with his first girl, and he tipped his head to look up at her. Her legs spread across his thighs, she was beautiful, erotically woman. Chestnut hair as dark as her eyes curled over her bare shoulders, hiding her breasts. He exposed them, her body lush and shapely and taunting his patience. This was a woman he never thought to have in his bed, to want to share so much with her—much more than his body. He sat up suddenly, gripping her hips and urging her closer to his heat.

She slid wetly against him, creating friction and slick impatience and delicious sensations that left him weak and pliable. And growling for more.

Madison loved it. Like a mighty rock tower torn to the ground, she manipulated him, teased him. His eyes slammed shut, his long, lean body glistening with sweat despite the cool air. She licked a trickle at his temple, whispering what she was feeling, how warm and solid he was for her and what that did to her. He groaned, hitting the bottom of his control.

"Madison, darlin'—" He showered quick, thick kisses over her throat and breasts. "Come to me."

She held his gaze, held him in her palm, and Alex experienced a trembling moment, a deeper intimacy as she slipped on the condom. They were never more together than in this instant. Here she trusted him.

Here she was his. If for one night or one month or
longer, he didn't know, didn't trust himself to think
beyond this moment. Only that she wanted him as
much as he did her.

He pushed himself inside her, barely. She was incredibly tight, and he teased the bead of her sex, waiting for her body to adjust, yet she spread her legs
wide, forced him deeper, then in one sharp motion,
she took control and thrust downward, gasping as he
filled her completely. He groaned her name, quaking
at the incredibly snug feel of her surrounding him.
Alex kissed her tenderly, his throat suddenly tight as
he tried understanding why it felt perfectly natural to
be inside her. As if he'd waited his lifetime to be right
here, right now.

Madison buried her face in his shoulders, the tiniest
tinge of pain passing and giving her a strange freedom. She smiled, met his gaze and wished she understood the look on his face.

"Ready to rock, rich boy," she whispered in
Alex's ear, and he choked a laugh, then went silent
as she rose and fell, taking and receiving him. He
wanted to lie back and watch, yet didn't want any
distance between them. Cupping her breasts, he rolled
the tips between thumb and forefinger, ducking to
suckle and lave. He teased the bead of her sex, watching her rock, watching the desire play over her face,
in her soft smile, until it was too much. He pulled her
legs around him and rolled her to her back. Locking
his fingers in hers and bracing himself, he retreated
and plunged, his gaze never wavering from hers. Her
body glistened and her hips rose to greet him, her
gaze sweeping briefly to where they joined before
meeting his again.

He withdrew and her legs grabbed him back, demanding he hide nothing, spare nothing. Then she told him so, and Alex was delirious with her, her scent and touch—her hotly whispered words.

Her soft yielding flesh gripped.

Her breath tumbled into his mouth and he drank it.

Her body pulsed, a savage claim to his tired soul.

And she begged for more.

Suddenly he swept her off the bed and against him, wrapping himself in her smooth muscled limbs. He shoved harder and harder, answering her pleas, holding her tight as she slammed and pushed and took from him all he could give.

Raw and piercing.

Slick skin and blistering heat. Wild, ravishing.

Her breath skipped.

He breathed her name, desperate, hungry.

Gripping his shoulders she bowed back, grinding to him as thick waves of pleasure swam through him. She flexed beautifully and trembled, a sight to behold, and he thrust and joined her climax, hot, pumping, an untamed blast through his blood. He held her suspended, watching rapture spear her, then taper off with her breathing. He didn't want it to stop, wanted to see her smile like that for an eternity. She straightened slowly, coming into his arms and sighing against him like a drape of silk.

Alex gasped and clutched her, raining kisses over her face, holding her sculpted jaw as if she'd suddenly vanish. "Madison, oh, darlin'—" His voice broke a bit, and he swallowed.

"I know," she whispered, tightening her arms and legs around him. She laid her cheek to his shoulder as he rocked her gently. Against his skin she smiled.

Alex squeezed his eyes shut, squeezing her, his pounding heart telling him they shared a power that went beyond this bed, this moment. And it scared him as well as comforted, called to him. "I was right," he said after several moments. "You're an addiction."

She lifted her head to look at him.

"I can't believe after that earth-shattering experience—" he watched her smile widen "—I could still want you again." He grunted. "But my knees are killing me." She laughed and he scooted to the edge of the bed. She left his lap, slipping into the nearby bathroom. Alex followed. She was already stepping into the shower.

He disposed of the condom and paused. There was a streak of blood on his thigh, and something gripped his chest.

"Madison?"

He opened the shower door and met her gaze.

Her guilty flush told him all he needed. "Why didn't you tell me you were a virgin?"

"You didn't need to know."

"How can you say that?" He stepped under the spray with her, his arms circling her. "Maddy! That's not something a woman gives up easily."

"I didn't." She cradled his face, staring into his eyes. "It was a wonderful experience, Alexander. One I'm certain I'll never forget, and it would have been different if you knew."

"Hell, yes. We weren't exactly…tame."

"Yeah, ain't it cool?" Madison grinned. He didn't. Oh dear, he wasn't taking this well.

"Did I hurt you?"

"You can do that to me all night."

He lowered his arms. "I don't think so."

Her expression fell. "*That's* why I didn't say anything." She rinsed and stepped past him.

Alex let the hot spray cover him like the guilt swimming through his blood. Part of him wondered if she expected anything from him now, and another part was so incredibly humbled he was gasping for air. He was the first man to touch her, be inside her, and he had the ridiculous urge to roar. Madison wasn't a careless woman. She didn't do anything she didn't want. Not until he'd cornered her into this lie with Angus. But when it came to them, no, she'd already proven she couldn't be easily swayed. And that she'd *wanted* to give that gift to him left him feeling unworthy of her.

He rinsed and left the shower, drying and slipping into a terry robe. He found her on the deck, a glass of wine in her hand. She stared out into the night-cloaked scenery below, wearing that silky creation that shaped her body and made him remember what her skin felt like in his hands, remember every subtlety of her climax. His body reacted with embarrassing swiftness, yet he felt strangely uncomfortable, especially after the abandon they'd just shared.

"Don't feel guilty, Alex. It wasn't your choice. It was mine."

"Why?"

Facing him, Madison met his gaze. *Because I'm falling in love with you,* she thought. She'd been tumbling since they'd danced in the moonlight and he wanted to be a true Southerner. But he wasn't ready to hear that and might never be. If he'd considered a relationship an hour ago, the look on his face was as closed as it had ever been. She felt suddenly very alone.

"Because I wanted to make love with you." She tipped the glass to her lips. "It's that simple."

"There is nothing simple about you, Madison." It came out sharper than he'd wanted.

She drained the wine. "Why are you so concerned? You've been with enough women to have had a least one virgin in the pile."

"No. Never." He moved until he felt the heat of her skin through her satin robe. "I haven't been with a woman in three years."

She blinked, then a little smile curved her lips. So, there weren't other women. "For a man, that's about like a recycled virgin, huh?"

He chuckled softly, shaking his head and sighing as he gathered her to him. "Yeah, I guess it is." He pressed a kiss to her temple. "I don't know what to say, baby. I'm honored, but—"

She met his gaze, covering his lips with two fingers. She didn't want him excusing away those precious moments. "I didn't make love with you to trap you or give you a guilt trip, Alexander. You're reading far too much into this. It was a burden as much as a gift." She lowered her hand to his shoulder. "And I wanted you. There can't possibly be any mistake in that."

His look was sly. "I think that's why it was such a shock. You didn't act like a virgin."

"This is the nineties, you know. Nineteen, not eighteen. With movies and literature, it's hard not to be educated." She cocked her head and in a Southern accent thicker than her own said, "Or would you rather I simply swoon, sah?"

His smile grew as she spoke. Madison, he realized, was a woman who did not dwell on the past long and moved on. "I would rather you kiss me."

"Oh-h, much obliged, sah."

And she did, her mouth driving him crazy, her body calling to be fondled, and she let him. In the dark, on the deck, she left him with no doubt that a twenty-five-year-old virgin was better than a woman with loads of experience.

An hour later they fell into the bed in a tumble of arms and legs and a lake of wrinkled sheets. Alex snuggled her into the curve of his body, yet before they settled, she reached for the phone.

"Room service?"

Alex leaned over her, smiling.

"Yes, cookies and milk, please." She met his gaze. "For two."

Alex looked up from his laptop and sank back into the chair, his chest constricting at the sight of her in the bed. She lay sprawled on her stomach, her hair spilling over her face and bare shoulders, the slender dip of her spine exposed where the sheet wrapped around her hips and buttocks.

He wanted to crawl in beside her, but after last night he understood she'd be a little tender. His brows furrowed, uncertainty sprinting through him. He'd woken twice during the night to simply stare at her, wondering why he hadn't recognized her innocence, then realized she wasn't, her sophistication shielding the fact that she'd never known another man.

*She's never known another man.*

His heart wrenched in his chest at the thought. Half with guilt, half with utter joy. He didn't deserve her.

She'd made it clear what she wanted, and he wasn't ready for that. He wasn't. Her virginity was a complication he hadn't foreseen, and though she absolved him of any responsibility, Alex couldn't shake the lingering guilt. He took a sip of coffee, closing his eyes. He had too many irons in the fire to consider a future, yet the image of her holding that baby kept flying through his mind like a whispering angel. He shook his head and straightened, setting the coffee aside and focusing on his computer.

"Why didn't you wake me?"

His gaze flew to her as she left the bed, careless of her nudity.

He looked his fill before he said, "Cover up, darlin', or you'll stay like that all day."

Smiling, almost daring him, she slipped into a robe, then belted it as she crossed the room to him.

For a moment they stared before she leaned down and brushed her mouth over his. The fire ignited quickly and he pulled her onto his lap, opening her robe and filling his palm with her breast as he kissed her.

Madison sank into the feel of him, loving his hands on her body, loving the innocence she shed last night in his arms. Though she'd nothing to compare it to, she knew no woman could ask for a better introduction. And she wanted another lesson, the center between her thighs growing quickly damp and pulsing.

She took his hand, pushing it there.

Alex smiled against her lips. He loved that she wasn't shy about her wants, and toyed with her, parting the soft curls and...

The cell phone rang.

She moaned a complaint.

He drew back, reaching for it. "I have to get it," he said regretfully, then opened the phone. She tried slipping from his lap, but he stopped her, kissing her softly as he put the phone to his ear. "Donahue," he said against her mouth, then jerked back. "Elizabeth!"

She stiffened, trying not to frown.

"How did you get this number?"

Madison listened to the one-sided conversation, feeling like an intruder. When she left his lap this time, he let her go.

"Destroy the number. This is for business only." A pause and then, "I know you didn't, darlin'—"

Madison felt her insides jerk at the endearment.

"—I can't take social calls right now."

Alex's gaze swung to Madison. She was sitting on the sofa, her legs curled to the side as she finished off her croissant. Her expression was blank as she dusted her fingertips.

"No, I'm not alone."

She met his gaze.

"It has nothing to do with you. It's...business."

Her heart did a painful drop just then. Business?

"Goodbye, Elizabeth." He clicked off the phone, staring at it for a moment before sliding a glance to her.

"You weren't very kind, Alex."

"I don't want to talk about her."

"I see."

"No, I don't think you do. She's just a friend."

Madison stood, walking toward the bathroom. "Get a reality check, Yankee. A friend doesn't hunt you down on your private line just to chat. Especially when she knows she shouldn't.'' She slipped into the bathroom.

"I'll change the number. I can't have Elizabeth thinking she can butt into my privacy when she wants.''

"Then you should have set her straight from the start.'' At his confused look, she gave him a playful shove. "She wants you.''

He scoffed. "She needs another dinner partner.''

"That's hardly it.''

"And I'm sure you are going to tell me,'' he said, slipping his arms around her and clasping his hands at the small of her back. The position said he would wait just like that till she had her say.

"She wants to marry you.''

His brows shot up. "Liz? She worries about her social calendar and whether or not she'll need a face-lift in ten years, but not marriage.''

"You're fooling yourself.''

He chucked under her chin, forcing her to meet his gaze. "What's this really about?''

"Why didn't you tell her you were with me?''

He didn't mistake the hurt in her voice. "It's none of her business. And I want to keep you to myself.''

"Or hidden.''

He frowned. "You can't believe that.''

"We both didn't want this relationship to be public. And before, it was understandable, but now?''

"You going to admit to being with me and risk becoming the flavor of the week?''

"Can I take out an ad? A billboard will do. Or maybe I'll just give the info to Bubba Pickney and heck, it'll be all over the South in about a week.''

His smile grew as she spoke. "I'll take that as a yes."

"Smart man." She kissed him lightly. "I'm not afraid of what anyone will say." *Because I love you too much,* she thought, fighting the urge to tell him.

"I know, but I don't want anyone hounding you, and I don't want them finding out what we've been doing here. I couldn't stand it if anyone thought less of you because of me and my mistakes."

Madison understood. If anyone got wind of this fake marriage, their reputations, hers especially, would be shot to pieces.

Alex sighed, jamming his hand into his hair and raking it back. Damn Elizabeth. If he didn't know better he'd believe she had a spy watching him. And he didn't want to tell anyone about Madison. Not because he wanted to keep this relationship secret, but because he was afraid the world he lived in would crush it with its ugliness. He didn't want to think about Savannah and what would happen when they returned. He ignored his uncertainty, ignored the goading voice inside him that asked if he was ready to go the distance and risk failing again—the voice that sounded too much like Celeste's.

# Ten

The beach was deserted, the evening air cool.

Alex sat behind her, his chest bracing her back as she sat between his legs on a flat rock, watching the sun go down. They shared a very expensive bottle of wine, drinking from the neck like Vikings. "This is so bohemian." She handed him the bottle.

He nuzzled her ear, whispering, "Your words are slurring," before tipping the bottle to his lips.

"I know." She tilted a look at him. "Quick. Take advantage of me."

He winked. "I will."

Madison didn't think she could be happier. They spent their days with the O'Malleys, pretending to be husband and wife and the night alone, exploring each other, ending a night of lovemaking with milk and cookies.

She tipped her head to look at him, the wind off

the lake tearing loose her hair and she brushed it back. "You look pensive."

He smiled down at her. "That's because my butt hurts sitting on these rocks."

She stood, pulling him to his feet and on the deserted stretch of shore, she slipped her hands inside his back jean pockets. She rubbed.

He moaned a little. "Now something else hurts."

"I can fix that, too."

"You're gonna kill me." She was insatiable and he loved it.

"Guess I need a new man, then." She stepped out of his arms and headed up the nearest slope.

He grabbed her, yanking her back and together they tumbled to the sand. "Am I that, Maddy? Your man?" His breath snagged in his chest as he waited.

"Yeah." With both hands, she fingered back his hair. "For as long as you want to be." She couldn't ask for more.

"As long as I can." Alex kissed her, pulling her around him, molding her body as if to bring her into himself. "Why is it always *right now* that I have to have you? Let's find some privacy." Climbing to their feet, they scrambled up the incline, racing across the avenue and into the inn. Minutes later, Alex's hand shook as he shoved in the key. She was already unbuttoning his shirt. The door opened and they fell inside, fell back against the door, tearing at each other's clothes, toeing off shoes and socks.

The shirts went, then her bra. And he cupped her breasts, sinking to take her nipple into his mouth. He ravished and tugged, and she clutched him closer, harder. He lowered to his knees, taking her panties down with her shorts.

He cupped her buttocks and pulled her under the warmth of his mouth. She shrieked and he chuckled, the sound vibrating through her being like a rumble of sweet thunder. He peeled her wider and laved the bud of her sex until she was begging for him to stop. He straightened but she was on him, pushing him to the floor. She jerked on his belt, opened his jeans and freed him.

"Now, Alex." She rocked against his thickness.

"Slow down." His hands roamed wildly over her skin.

"I can't."

"But we need a— Tell me there's a condom in this thing." He dumped her purse on the floor, scattering the contents. He found one.

It was on and he was inside her in one plunging stroke. "Oh, that's heaven, heaven." He withdrew and shoved. "I'm sorry."

"Don't be. More." She locked her legs around him and met his thrusts, begged for his strength. She whispered in his ear how much she loved this wild impatient side of him. For it matched hers.

"You make me crazy," he said into her mouth as he pushed and pushed, moving her across the floor. "Oh, Maddy."

"Alex!"

"Yeah, honey, I feel it. Show me, show me." He cradled her head in his palms and withdrew and thrust, watching her passion explode over her features, feel it ripple though her lithe body and into his. It was exquisite, heart wrenching and he pushed once more and joined her, bodies straining, grinding to keep the last vestiges of desire within. They trembled,

kisses calming to tenderness and together they started
breathing hard and laughing.

"Remind me never to drink wine with you."

"Felt different this time, huh?" he said. As if there
was nothing between them.

"Yeah." She stroked damp locks from his forehead. "But then it feels incredible every time you
ravish me."

All morning before the cermony for Angus and
Laura, Madison felt suddenly, coldly, locked out,
minutes after a phone call woke him just after dawn.
He'd been working nonstop since, talking on the
phone to Kyle, Steven Reynolds, even Anna Marsh.
That he didn't confide in her wasn't a concern. She
knew little of his business and didn't care to know,
but that he tipped the computer screen away when
she was near, or talked softly enough for her to get
the message that the call was confidential, didn't escape her. Stinging a little, she gave him privacy and
had waited patiently on the deck till it was time to
leave for Angus's home. She didn't want to think
about Elizabeth's call, but it plagued her like a dis-
ease. Yet even now, Madison recognized the tension
in his shoulders, his punishingly straight spine in the
upholstered seat of the rented Jaguar. His fingers
flexed on the steering wheel as they drove to the
O'Malleys' lake house. She knew how much Little
People meant to him, and she wished she could help
him, do anything to erase the serious look on his
handsome face. Yet she wondered if his concern had
to do with Elizabeth or his deal with Angus.

He pulled into the drive and turned off the motor,

staring for a long moment over the sloping hood. "I'm sorry."

"For what?"

He turned his head and met her gaze. "Ignoring you."

"You aren't my happiness guru, Alex."

His lips quirked.

"I've been living alone for a while. And I like my own company."

"So do I."

Together they leaned, and the instant her hands touched his shoulders, grinding away the tightness, Alex moaned.

"Let me make it better, Yankee," she whispered, before her mouth covered his.

Alex responded like a crazed animal, sudden and fiery, cradling her face in his palms and tasting her. *Oh, no, I can't lose this,* he thought as fresh desire rocketed through him.

"Feeling better?"

"Uh-uh, need some more therapy." He worried her lips, his tongue outlining their lush shape before pushing deeply inside. She purred for him, twisting in the seat to get closer to him, her hands pulling at his shoulders and pulling him down.

"Do these seats go back?"

Alex nearly howled at the image she created. "I don't think Angus would take too kindly to his guests making love in his driveway."

"We could leave, go down to the lake. No one knows we're here yet."

"You tempt me, woman," he said, whispering kisses over her throat, then lower.

"That's the idea." She'd rather be naked with him

than watching Angus and Laura renew their vows. It was just lousy timing, but she didn't need the emotions of a wedding giving Alex the wrong idea about her. What she'd said earlier was the truth. He wasn't responsible for her happiness. But right now she was damn happy to be kissing him and held him completely responsible for the pleasure.

Childish giggles came to them, and Alex looked up, scanning the area.

"We're surrounded."

"Do we take cover or fight them off?"

He met her gaze. "Take no prisoners."

She rolled her eyes. "Typical man. I say we go for negotiations." She sat up, giving a mock scowl to the kids before she opened the car door.

"We don't have anything to bargain with, do we?"

She reached behind the seat and pulled out a bag, grinning like Santa on Christmas, before leaving the car. Children surrounded her, and she doled out prizes they'd won from the festival, saving the last stuffed rabbit for Shannon.

"Young'uns, gotta love 'em," she said as they scattered like mice.

Alex felt a pinch of guilt as he lifted the brightly wrapped gifts and came around to the side of the car. He recognized the longing in her dark eyes as she watched the children, knew she wanted some of her own. Babies, the mere thought of them, terrified him and though she didn't look the least bit maternal in the curve-hugging raspberry suit, he couldn't help thinking what a wonderful mother she'd make. And that she would be having children with another man. His heart clenched just then, and he turned his attention to the sprawling estate, wanting to get lost somewhere with her, yet knowing his future lay in Angus O'Malley's hands. He had to be here. Sliding his arm around her waist, he walked with her toward the house, dread moving over his spine.

The moment they stepped through the front door of the O'Malleys' lake house, Colleen, Bridgett and Megan ushered Madison off to the upper floor. She looked back over she shoulder at him, shrugging, then going along.

"What's this all about?"

Randy smiled as the women helped his wife up the stairs. "Hell if I know. Weddings are for women, right? Even renewals. But then, you know that already. Men are supposed to arrive clean shaven for the sacrifice." Randy gave his shoulder a commiserating shake. "Don't tell my wife I said that, 'cause marrying her was the best thing that ever happened to me. And she knows it."

Alex gave him a side glance and wished he understood, then knew he was beginning to, slowly.

"Come on, Angus wants to talk to you."

A tightness formed in Madison's throat at the sight of Laura in her wedding gown. The forty-year-old creation was lacy and demure, and as Madison stood with the other guests as Angus and Laura promised another forty years with each other, she felt a tinge of envy. Her parents would have celebrated their thirtieth this month. To last forty years, she thought, when people married and divorced with such ease, was a remarkable occasion.

She could imagine Angus and Laura years before, a strapping Irishman and his bonny bride. Angus had said he'd owned no more than a box of tools and the

clothes on his back. It was how her father had come
to her mother. Penniless, with only his love. Her eyes
burned suddenly, and she wished she and Alex had
met under different circumstances. But the reality was
it wouldn't have mattered. She would still love him.
She heard the precious vows and realized she would
never have this with the man she loved.

She was in love alone.

After the ceremony she thanked Laura for including her and Alex in their happiness and moved off.
A pair of nannies had been hired to care for the children while the mothers prepared, and Madison left
Shannon in loving arms before searching out Alex.
She found him leaning against a tree, his dark suit
clashing against the white flowers and blue ribbons
woven around the trunk.

"What's wrong?"

Alex looked at her, his brows knit tightly. "Angus
offered for us to renew our vows with them."

She inhaled, her eyes flying wide. "What did you
say?"

"I told him we didn't want to take away from this
special day for them."

She let out a deep sigh. "Good. Because I will only
carry this lie so far. Marriage is sacred. I don't like
being a phony, especially today."

Tension skipped up his spine. "He was pretty
hopeful."

"Then tell him the truth."

"I can't. Not for me, but…God, Madison." He
looked away. "I wish I'd never started this."

Her expression softened, and she stepped closer.
"It's okay. Without a license it wouldn't be legal,
anyway."

"Yeah, I guess so," he said, looking at the lake and wondering why his chest suddenly burned.

"We'd have a devil of a time keeping it secret, regardless."

He turned his head.

"The last thing I want is to let the media trap us into something we don't want."

He didn't speak, bracing his shoulder on the tree and meeting her gaze.

"You and I might be having fun now, Alex, but this isn't real."

He scowled. "It was real as hell last night when I was inside you, and you were screaming for more."

She smiled and tilted her head. "Oh, darling, that's not what I'm saying." She slipped closer, brushing a lock of hair off his brow, and Alex closed his eyes briefly, loving the constant gesture. "We're in an artificial world here, far away from friends and the public eye. I know you don't want this to get out of hand when we return, and neither do I."

"Are you saying when we get home, it's over?"

*God no,* he thought.

"Uh-uh, Yankee, you aren't getting away that easily." His shoulders sagged with relief, and Madison felt her heart skip with hope. "I'd like us to go on forever, but you made your future plans clear."

His gaze narrowed. "I feel a very ugly *but* coming."

"I've got you here, all to myself, without too many distractions, but in Savannah, with your company, your social calendar, the press—" she made a face on that one "—it's different. And you know it. I'm afraid you won't have room for anything else."

"That's not all of it. You don't think I can commit to a relationship."

"How can you? You're so committed to your work, look where its led you...and me."

"What if I say I've been thinking differently—"

"Shh, no, darling, don't think so much." She pressed against him, and his arm slid smoothly around her waist. "I adore you, Alexander, truly I do. But don't try to convince yourself that you have to want what I do to be happy." She cupped his jaw, gazing deeply into his eyes. "I *am* happy, just the way we are." She brushed her mouth across his, and Alex had barely the chance to trace her lips with his own before she walked away.

A month ago, that's exactly what he wanted to hear. Was relieved to hear. But now he felt ostracized from her, warned. They might be good together beyond the bedroom, but she didn't believe in him. Not where it counted. Not in matters of the heart. Alex knew he'd no one to blame, except himself. He'd put up so many roadblocks, she didn't believe there was any way in. And now, she had some of her own.

Alex looked at her and saw the soft sheen of tears as her gaze followed Angus and Laura.

"Madison?"

"I want to go home. I can't do this anymore."

In the hotel room he moved to the desk, racking papers, organizing notes, yet he could feel her without looking, smell her scent as she passed him and went to her bags. He packed up his laptop, smirking to himself when he found a foil packet underneath. They must have used dozens of these, he thought, shoving it into his pocket. Finally he looked at her. His insides ground as she unpinned her hair, fluffing out the long, brown curls, and he wished he could say something, but the words wouldn't come. The inability shamed him, leaving him feeling raw and aching and lonely.

She selected a traveling outfit and started undressing, kicking off her heels.

Alex felt time slipping away. He closed the briefcase and went to her.

She stilled, meeting his gaze, her suit jacket open and exposing her breasts cupped in raspberry lace.

They stared.

"What?"

"I wish I could make the world go away."

She laid her hand to his chest. "It will be all right, Alex. You'll get the company and be richer than ever." She tried to smile and failed.

"That's not what I meant."

He ducked, his mouth swooping down on hers, his arms locking around her. She responded instantly, pushing her fingers into his hair and arching to the bend of his body. He lifted her, and she wrapped her legs around his hips, kissing him harder, hungrier, her hand wedged between them and opening his trousers.

Her hand dove inside, fingers closing, stroking, and he dropped to the edge of the bed, stripping off her jacket, unfastening her bra. His mouth was on her in an instant, swallowing her nipple, sucking it deeply as his hand worked under her skirt, feeling past the stockings and garters to the thong he knew she wore. He pulled the panties aside, probing.

Her breath scattered over his face, her silken muscles flexing, and he knew she was as close to the edge as he was.

"Alex. Hurry." She shoved his clothing down and climbed higher.

Alex dug in his pocket for the foil. She took it, tore the packet open with her teeth, then rolled it down.

"Madison, honey—" he groaned as she guided him inside her.

She slammed into him, pushing him down on the bed and riding him. Raw, primitive. Alex rolled her to her back and shoved, and she smiled, meeting his thrusts, clutching him harder.

"I adore what you do to me, my love," she whispered.

My love. "Oh, Madison, you humble me." He rained kisses over her face, pushing and pushing, trying to grab more of her, keep her closer, longer. Here they trusted and here he wanted to stay. But sensations crested, broke free too soon. And they bowed against each other, fused, fingers digging into skin, bodies clenching and flexing as rapture flooded through them, melting two into one. They lay suspended for seconds, then sank together to the bed, still joined, still kissing with all the heat of moments before.

Holding his gaze, she smoothed his hair back, her breathing rushed.

His gaze searched hers, seeking he didn't know what. Only that he was desperate to keep her and didn't know how to do it.

"I'm not going anywhere, Alexander."

He let out a long breath, then buried his face in the curve of her shoulder. She could read his mind, he swore. "Madison—I—" He stalled, swallowing. "I need you."

She closed her eyes tightly, sending a tear rolling

sideways to her temple. She knew it was hard for him to admit even that and she wished she had the nerve to tell him how madly she loved him. She opened her eyes, her gaze catching the flicker of light off her diamond ring as she stroked his hair. "I need you, too."

But the instant they set foot in Savannah, being his sometimes wife would be over.

# Eleven

Alex stared out the window in his offices, his hands clasped behind his back. He wanted to ignore the woman standing opposite his desk, but he knew the confrontation had been a long time coming. He and Madison had managed to slip into the city unnoticed and enjoy nearly two weeks without the press or anyone else infringing on their privacy. He'd done his best to keep it that way, and though he'd taken her out only a few times, that had been their undoing. Word traveled too fast and he didn't want anything to get back to Angus and spoil the deal that was days away. They were both back to the real world, Madison caring for a widower's children and he...well, he was confronting his mistakes again.

"Are you at least going to look at me?"

"We have nothing to say to each other, Elizabeth."

"You're upset that I called you when you were on your little vacation. I said I was sorry."

"You lied to my secretary. You nearly cost Parrish her job."

"I just wanted to talk with you."

"So talk."

"Not when you're this…cold."

He turned his gaze from the view of the harbor. "I haven't changed, Liz."

"Yes, you have. I saw you in town with her. Everyone did. But they don't know what I know."

Alexander faced her fully. "And that is?"

"You're married, aren't you?"

His shoulders tensed. "No."

"You're wearing a ring, Alex. Like hers."

He glanced down at the band. He hadn't taken it off yet. He couldn't, as if doing so would unravel his life with Madison. "It's just a ring."

"Then why on that finger? And did you register as Mr. and Mrs. Donahue just to shack up for a couple of weeks of hot sex?"

Alex's features went taut. She'd had him investigated. "Damn you."

"Is it true?"

Alex refused to respond.

"No, you'd never marry. Not even for good sex."

"Don't be vulgar, Liz."

Liz's gaze slid between the look on his face and the ring he twisted. "Why were you her lover and not mine?"

He stared her down. "This conversation is over, Elizabeth."

Suddenly she was close. "What is she to you? I have a right to know."

"We're...friends."

Further words snagged in his throat as he looked past Liz to Madison standing in the doorway, his secretary behind her.

Liz twisted, smiling thinly and running her hand down his chest before she stepped away.

"Maddy," he said, moving around the desk and coming to her. The look on her face made him stop in his tracks.

Madison fought the hole digging in her heart and searched his gaze, his handsome features. "Friends, Alexander?"

He glanced briefly at Liz. "Not now, Maddy."

It hit her then. Really hit her. They'd been together most of the time since returning from Michigan. He worked out of his home, picked her up after work. Not because they didn't want their marital status to get back to Angus, but because Alex wasn't ready to admit to anyone, even to the one person he should, that they had a relationship. A very loving, honest relationship. Until now.

Liz glanced between the two, hiding her smile. "I'll see you later, Alex."

"No." Madison said, without taking her gaze from Alexander's. "Don't bother. I'll go." She turned on her heels and left.

Alex was stunned motionless.

"I knew it," Liz said. "I knew you didn't want what she had to offer."

Alex's features pulled tight, and he bolted from the office, skidding to a halt before the elevators. She was already inside, and the doors were closing. *"Madison."*

She didn't speak, her wound so clear in her eyes.

A tear fell. Alex swore he heard his heart fracture. The door hushed closed.

He didn't lose her. He didn't. He wouldn't let it happen. She was in for a surprise if she thought she could leave him without a fight.

The timer binged. Madison jolted up from where she lay curled on the sofa, blinking first at Kat, then the table between them. "A drumroll please," she muttered, and together they leaned over the glass table to stare at the plastic stick. Positive. "Wonderful." Madison flopped into the sofa. A baby. Alex's baby. The thought of holding his child inside her sent unbelievable joy through her. And sadness. She was on her own.

Katherine settled in the Louis XIV chair with all the elegance of his queen. "You don't look that upset."

Madison stared out the window, not seeing the flat, grassy land leading to the best deep-water view in Savannah. "I'm not. I was hoping my suspicions weren't true, is all. Dang. We used tons of protection."

"Apparently one of those icky things broke."

A little smile curved her lips when she thought of the times making love with him was so vigorous it was entirely possible. Especially the night they'd drunk wine on the beach.

"You're not going to tell him, are you?"

Madison looked down at her hands clenched in her lap. She'd been on her way to his office to tell him her suspicions when she'd heard him tell Liz… "No. I won't."

Katherine frowned. "That's not fair to Alex."

"I can't. He'd insist on marrying me because of a baby and resent me and our child for forcing him into a corner." Her voice broke. "I couldn't bear that."

"I think you underestimate his feelings for you."

Madison turned her gaze on Katherine.

"I've seen him a few times since you returned from Michigan. Everyone is talking about the changes in him. Until a couple of days ago, he wore a sappy smile he couldn't wipe off."

That was a comfort, but she had to be realistic. "He'd made it perfectly clear what he wanted, Kat. I understood that going in. That scene only proved it." Her voice wavered again, and she swallowed. "I'm trying to respect his preferences, when I'd rather scream to the heavens how much I love him." She cocked her head. "You know he rarely asked about my family. It's like he didn't want to dig too deep. Or get involved any more than what he could handle on a temporary basis."

"Well then, I guess you aren't going to like this any more than the Mercedes." When Madison wouldn't answer his calls, Alex had done what a millionaire did well, he'd sent her a gift. A new Mercedes delivered to her door. She'd sent it back with an envelope. In it was the diamond ring she'd worn while playing his wife.

Madison felt dread dip through her as Kat twisted to the side table and slipped a paper free from her planner. She leaned forward to hand it to her.

Madison stared at her Wife Incorporated statement and the six-figure deposit he'd made in her account. "Damn him."

The next morning she hadn't calmed yet as she strode into his corporate office and slapped the paper on his desk. "Explain this."

He didn't have to look. "I paid you as I would any person, lawyer or financier—" he shrugged "—who'd helped me get that company." His heart had jumped to life the instant she'd stepped inside and was now beating furiously. Even if she was spitting mad.

"You might as well have left twenty dollars on the nightstand."

Instantly his look turned black. "Don't cheapen what we have."

She shook the bank draft. "You did!"

Remorse cloaked his features, and he moved around the edge of the desk, slowly, because she looked like a doe about to bolt. "I'm sorry. I did it to get you here, Maddy and you need the money, I know you do."

"Not from you. I was a banker, Alex. I can take care of myself. I work for Wife Incorporated because I *want* to, because I'm good at it. This—" she flicked the draft "—tells me what I've ignored because of my feelings for you. We don't want the same things. We don't even *see* the same things, or you would have told the truth about us to Liz."

"She already knew."

"That doesn't matter. She was as much the public eye as a newspaper—and if you want to play it safe, then fine..." Madison's eyes burned, her heartache stealing her breath. "Play alone."

Alex's heart slammed against the wall of his chest. "No, dammit." He hesitated, grinding his hand over his face. "I don't want to end this, Maddy."

She shook her head. "You don't have a choice.

The first chance you had, you gave me up like a sacrifice, rather than admit we were lovers. I don't want to be the best-kept secret in Savannah.''

That sounded like a threat. "And you think a proposal will change that?''

"No, not from you." She turned toward the door.

Panic seized him. "What do you expect from me?''

She glanced. "Did I ever demand anything from you?''

She hadn't. She only gave. "No expectations. We agreed.''

Her gaze narrowed, her temper rising as she faced him. "Right, we did. And now, don't expect anything from me, Alexander. I don't want your high-priced crumbs.''

His features tightened, and he felt backed into a corner. "Did you give me your virginity so when the push came, I'd feel guilty enough to marry you?''

Hurt clutched at her throat. Tears burned her eyes.

Alex realized his carelessness an instant before she slapped him.

The imprint of her hand reddened on his tanned cheek as she tore the bank draft in two, then turned away.

"Madison—I—" Alex cursed foully. What had gotten into him to say that!

She threw the shredded paper back over her shoulder as she strode from his office.

He dropped into his leather chair and swung toward the view, a profound and cutting sadness ripping through his chest. He leaned forward, bracing his elbows on his knees, his hands over his face. *Oh, God. What have I done?*

And why didn't he go after her?

* * *

Alex had told himself this was what he wanted. Safe. Life with boundaries. Except he was coming apart at the seams, the ache in his chest increasing as the days passed. He couldn't work, snapping at everyone, and he couldn't sleep—she walked through his dreams when she did. Tossing back a gulp of brandy, he relished the burn on its way to his stomach as he stared out the window. Even in the darkness, he could see the azaleas she'd planted in the garden. They'd argued mildly about it. He hadn't wanted them. She'd said he needed to join the living, that the condo looked as if no one lived here. It was never a home, not to him. He'd forgotten what home was until Madison showed him.

He rubbed his face and sighed. *God, this hurts.*

He glanced to the side, his gaze falling on a framed photo of her holding her fish and smiling like the sun. Just to look at her made his chest burn with pain. Beside that picture were more. She'd dug them out of an old storage box, pictures of his parents, of him as a child. She hadn't done it for herself, but for him. And it made him see that putting his heart in a box wouldn't protect himself from pain.

No, he thought, he'd brought that upon himself. Again. He'd betrayed her with cruel words. He'd pushed her away because he was afraid she had what he wanted, and he was too scared to take it. His throat tightened miserably and he sank into a chair. He missed her. Nothing filled the emptiness. Nothing ever would. He looked up at the phone, then went to it, dialing. A recording told him the number had been disconnected. Panicked, he called the operator for another listing. There wasn't one. Alex raced outside and drove to her apartment. A For Rent sign hung in the window. He rapped on the door, anyway. Then, standing on Gaston Street in the middle of the night, Alex felt the impact of how much he'd lost—and how deeply he could love.

She'd vanished. And very slowly he was going mad.

"Dammit, Katherine, tell me where she is."

"I can't. She asked me not to."

Alex ran his fingers though his hair as he paced before her desk. "I can't believe she'd cut me out like this."

He looked awful, dark rings under his eyes and she'd swear he'd slept in his clothes. If he slept at all. "She needs to be alone."

"I need her."

Katherine's heart clenched at the softly uttered words, hurt and lonely and in love. But he would be the last man to admit it aloud. She leaned forward, her elbows braced on the desk. "You could find her if you wanted."

"I do want! Good Lord, I've called and looked everywhere and," he stopped long enough to glare at her, "why didn't you tell me she was a partner with you in Wife Incorporated?"

"She's a silent partner. Ten percent. The dividends pay her bills, but don't keep her head that far above water."

What bills did she need to pay except her own? And it wasn't like Madison to run. But then, no one hurt her like he had.

Katherine rose from her chair and skirted the edge of her Queen Anne desk. "You wounded my friend deeply and to rail at you now would be rude, but Alexander, you apparently said some awful things."

He rubbed his face and sank miserably into the plush chair. "I practically accused her of trapping me."

"Oh, Alex."

Shame mapped his features. "I've ruined the best thing that's ever happened to me."

"Want some cheese with that whine?"

He lifted his gaze. "I don't need jokes. I need you to tell me where she is."

"I can't. I swore a Kappa Delta oath."

Alex had had enough. His future was at stake and he'd be damned if he'd let their sorority pact keep him from the woman he loved. He rose, looming over her petite form. "You either tell me, Katherine Beaucamp Davenport, or I will tell Cookie Ledbetter that Savannah's leading lady has a tattoo on her hip."

Her eyes flew wide. "You wouldn't dare!"

He arched a dark brow, the sharp snap of a raven's wing.

"You're that desperate you'd sully my reputation?"

"You got it."

# Twelve

**T**he deadline was up. Angus O'Malley was in town and prepared to sell. Timing couldn't be worse, Alex thought as he headed to his office, his steps hesitant. He didn't want to be here, not now.

"You look awful."

Alex jerked a look to the far end of his office, to the grouping of furniture artfully surrounded by palms. Angus rose from the sofa with his lawyers.

"I know. I apologize for the delay."

Angus inclined his head to his lawyers. The men departed quickly as Angus crossed to him.

Alex slung his briefcase onto the desk and sighed, raking his fingers through his neatly combed hair.

"What's the problem, son?"

Son. God, he could use his own father right now. He never felt so alone in his life. "There's something I need to tell you."

"That you're not married to Madison?"

His gaze flew to the old man's.

Angus smiled. "You don't think I'd sell my company to anyone without a thorough background check. I've known for some time."

"I apologize for lying, Angus. Madison—" he swallowed…it hurt just to say her name "—she didn't have anything to do with the lie. She helped me in a bad situation. I wanted this company badly and assumed if you thought I was married, you'd sell faster."

"I wouldn't give up my life's work to anyone else, son. Sean asked me not to."

Alex's eyes widened. "You knew my father?"

Angus nodded, recognizing the longing in the man's voice. "You're his image. It nearly killed me to be the one to take the company. And I've been watching you for years."

Alex's features tightened. "Why?"

"Your father and I…we started out the same, nothing but ideas and our tools. But we each had a little capital. If we'd been wise, we'd have pooled our resources and merged." He sent him a wry glance. "But we Irish tend to be too stubborn for our own good."

Alex smirked to himself.

"When Sean passed away, I felt obligated to watch over you, but knew you wouldn't accept help. And it was me who sent the lawyer to the jail when you were a kid."

"I always wondered how he'd found me." Alex rubbed his face, impatient to leave, to find Madison.

"I'm proud of you son, if that means anything."

Alex's throat clenched. "Yes, it does. I appreciate your saying so, Angus."

"So, what did you do to Madison?"

He looked at Angus, yet only saw the destroyed look on Madison's face when she'd slapped him. His chest constricted and he fell into the nearest chair, clutching his head. What a jerk he'd been. He'd no right to ask her forgiveness. But he had to. He felt barren and useless without her. He couldn't live like this. Not when he loved her more than his own life.

He loved her—truly, madly loved her. And the fear that it might be too late sent him out of the chair. "I can't buy your company, Angus. Thanks for the opportunity, but there are some things that are more important to me right now."

Alex didn't bother to say goodbye. He left the office at a dead run.

Angus smiled to himself. "Ah-h, laddie, you've finally learned."

Loud incessant hammering rudely woke her, and after mastering the threat of morning sickness, Madison went downstairs, silently complaining that it was just too dang early for house repairs. Although the place desperately needed them. She'd been gone for days, working hard, dragging herself in late last night after caring for a widower's children. She understood their pain, and her only comfort was that after trying to soothe their heartache and keeping them fed and moderately happy, their grandmother was with them now.

Claire looked up from the paper, then rose to pour her a cup of coffee. "Decaf."

Madison made a face, then sipped, wincing when the hammering started again. And the voices.

"Now, son, you got to level that first," her daddy said from somewhere close by.

"Sure, Davis, give me a hand? It's been a while."

The mug faltered in her hand, her heart pounding wildly as she stepped out onto the porch as Alex came around the side of the house with her father. Both men wore jeans and T-shirts, already sweating from the morning heat, and she tried not to notice Alex's smile. Or how much it hurt just to look at him. "I'm gonna kill Kat."

Every cell in Alex's body leaped to life, and he swore he could stand there for the rest of his life, just staring at her. Barefoot, wearing cut-off jeans and a Kappa Delta T-shirt, she never looked more beautiful. And unreceptive. "Actually, I blackmailed her." He laid the plank on the step and positioned it, his hand trembling a bit. He was so excited to see her, it took every ounce of willpower not to drag her into his arms and kiss the daylights out of her. "But she didn't give you up. I didn't know sorority pacts were so binding." He checked the level, not mentioning that Kat had given him a couple of hints.

"Then how did you find me?" Her daddy moved away.

He met her gaze, the festering wound in her eyes cutting through to his soul. "You should know by now I get what I want."

She scoffed. "You don't know what the hell you want, Alexander Donahue."

"Oh, yes, I do," he said with a long look, before he slammed the hammer and drove each nail home in one blow.

"Oh, yeah, a toy company."

Throwing down the hammer, he strode up the porch steps. Her pulsing stuttered with every step. "I didn't buy it." His gaze searched hers for the love she'd had, the love he'd ignored. He hoped to God it was still there.

"But you worked your whole life to get Little People."

"Angus knew we weren't married." He told her about their conversation. "I didn't want the toy company for me. You were right. I was so driven, I didn't see the world moving along without me. I'm to blame for Celeste going to another man. I'm to blame for ignoring everything for my quest of my father's dream. His. Not mine." He drew a long breath. "And I'm to blame for being so scared of losing anyone I cared about that I pushed you away before I realized how great I had it."

"I gave you what you wanted, Alex." Her voice broke. "How much do you have to hurt me before you're satisfied?"

Alex's heart sank. "I'm sorry, honey. I know I said some horrible things to you."

Her lip trembled and her eyes threatened tears. "You destroyed me."

His throat burned, and he stepped closer. "I was afraid. I couldn't admit to myself how I felt about you, really felt, let alone say it to Elizabeth."

She couldn't do this now and turned away, but from behind, he gripped her arms.

"Don't do this, baby," he whispered in her ear. "We have to work this out."

In the glass door, she stared at his reflection, her

throat closing with anguish. "We're too far apart, Alex."

"Not as far as you want to believe." He rubbed her arms.

She spun around. "Don't say you are ready, because you aren't ready for *me,* Alexander. You aren't." She exhaled, a tired sigh that cut through him. She looked exhausted and thin and weary. "Go home."

"My home is where you are." He leaned, bracing his hands on the door frame, hemming her in. He gazed deep into her eyes. "You can stand there and say you don't love me, but I can see it in your eyes. I can feel it every time you take a breath. I'm not leaving." His look was utterly belligerent. "So what are you gonna do about me?"

"I have a twelve-gauge."

He grinned. "That won't stop me."

"Alex." Her shoulders drooped. She couldn't think straight with him this close, smiling at her like that. "I don't need this right now."

"What do you need?" came tenderly. "Tell me, and I'll do it."

Her gaze flew to his. "All I ever wanted was the chance to love you."

"Then give me the chance, baby." He mashed her up against the wall, cupping her face between his palms. "I love you."

She searched his gaze, her heart in her throat.

"I love you, Madison." She shook her head, but he held her still. "I do love you. I can't eat, can't sleep, you walk through my dreams. What else do I have to do to make you believe I'm ready for this?"

"*This?* See, you can't even say it. Commitment,

Alexander. Marriage. You still act as if it's a death sentence. I don't want you that way, and you never asked.'' Pushing him back, she slipped into the house and closed the door.

Inside the house, Madison stood just behind the door, fighting tears and watching him through the window. She felt Claire move up behind her.

''Go to him, Maddy.''

''I can't.'' *He'll run when he finds out I'm pregnant,* she thought. Love, marriage and kids didn't always go together. She couldn't allow herself to hope.

''Yes, you can. All you have to do is forgive him.''

''It still hurts.''

''And only he can heal the pain. Let him do it.'' A pause and then, ''Don't you think that if I had a chance to be with Mitch I would? But he's dead. *Dead,*'' she snapped, and Madison flinched. ''But Alex is out there, waiting for his chance.''

Madison let out a shuddering breath. ''Pride is an ugly thing, isn't it, sister?''

''Yeah, and he's swallowing his for you.''

In the middle of the night, Madison felt the sheets slip away and she turned in the bed. A figure loomed in the shadows. ''Alex!'' she hissed.

''Glad you still recognize me in the dark,'' he whispered, pulling her into his arms. He kissed her, deep and thrilling, loving the greediness of her mouth on his.

She tore her mouth away. ''You can't do this. Daddy and Claire are—''

''Your father is spending the night with his woman in Bluffton, and Claire is over at her friend's place.''

She slept naked, and Alex took advantage. He bent, closing his lips around her nipple.

Her breath caught, then shuddered softly. "Unfair," she gasped as he drew the tender tip deeper into his mouth.

"I know."

She sank back, pulling him with her. "Oh, Alexander. I've missed you."

"I love you, Maddy. I love you so much it hurts. Let me show you."

She trembled with want and didn't argue, didn't think, letting her love for him show by her touch as she peeled off his clothes. His hands were never still, and before she could take a decent breath, he smothered the curves of her breasts with wet kisses, licked a path up her spine. He drew patterns over her tattoo of Yosemite Sam, telling her he wasn't going anywhere. Ever. Then he tasted her sweet center with long flowing strokes and felt her tremble, felt her heave and sigh and call his name as the pressure of desire swelled in her. She opened for him, pulling him down on top of her, and in one smooth motion he filled her, without anything between them, risking all and risking his heart to win her back. He absorbed her into him, calling her name, telling her how much he adored her and it was different than before because he loved, and different now because he knew it.

He told her he wanted her love back, wanted to marry her, make babies with her, and she cried in his arms. He held her close, feeling her body clench around him and gave a final push, watching her peaking pleasure explode over her features and grip him.

Nothing in his life was better than when she was holding him inside her.

"I love you, Alexander," she whispered into the curve of his ear. "I always will."

Alex closed his eyes, murmuring his love and absorbing the completion she made in his soul. But when he awoke sometime around dawn and reached for her, the warm spot beside him was empty. Then he heard a noise and flicked on the light. Leaving the bed, he pulled on his jeans, fitting his shirt over his head as he stopped outside the hall bathroom. "Madison?"

"Go away."

"Damn, honey, you keep saying that, and I'm going to get a complex."

"Please," she cried.

He opened the door and found her sitting on the floor, her back braced against the tile tub. She was pale as a sheet.

"You don't listen very well, do you?"

"What's going on?"

"Nothing." She tried to stand, but made it as far as her knees before she retched into the toilet. Alex soaked a washcloth and, kneeling, he pressed it to her flushed cheeks.

"You're pregnant."

"No kidding." She struggled to her feet, then rinsed her mouth and washed her face. He loomed behind her, his expression angry and disappointed.

"You were going to keep this from me." This is why she vanished so quickly.

"You didn't want a future. This—" she patted her tummy "—is a living, breathing future. I can handle this alone."

Her exclusion of him, after all they'd been through, sent his anger mounting, and he wanted to shake some sense into her. "You're being damned unfair, Madison. I love you. I wanted to marry you before I opened this door, but you had no right to keep this from me."

He forced her to look at him, his gaze ripping over her face. Then he kissed her, hard and compelling before he let her go, tucking in his shirt as he descended the stairs. Minutes later she heard his Jaguar peeling down the gravel drive, heading for the highway. Madison covered her face with her hands and slid to the floor.

He didn't come back. He didn't call. She was afraid she'd lost him for good. Three days passed before she heard anything, and it was from Kat.

"He did *what?*"

"He put up a billboard on Abercorn Street. It's mother huge, Mad. And it says, Alexander Donahue loves Madison Holt. With a plea to marry him. Every radio station is talking about it."

"Oh, Lord." A pleasant warmth seeped into her blood.

"He's adorably pitiful."

"Flowers, gifts—billboards. It's talk."

"Honey, it's shouting."

"Kat."

"Why, Maddy? You love him, don't you?"

"More than anything, but Alex can't change overnight."

"Hey, from what I've seen he's been changing all along. I've never seen the man so determined to get what he wants. And he wants you."

Her heart skipped. "I have to think of my family and this child."

"And when the hell are you going to just take what you want! You've been giving for so long, Maddy. It's your turn."

Oh, how she wanted desperately to take it all for herself. But she still had family obligations and couldn't ask Alex to take on the burden. Yet the nice, neat little package loomed ahead, and Madison wondered exactly what was stopping her. He loved her, wanted to marry her even before he knew of the baby. But she couldn't just abandon her family. Daddy needed her. Claire had another year of school left. *And you're scared to take the chance,* a voice pestered. *You're terrified that homegrown and simple isn't enough for Alexander.*

The sound of tires splattering gravel on the drive drew her attention, and she brushed back the curtain and saw a four-by-four ATV. "Someone's here. Probably made a wrong turn off the highway." She said goodbye and hung up. Kat's words ringing in her ears, she stepped out onto the porch.

Alex got out of the truck.

Her eyes widened and her pulse pounded as he marched up the steps, took her hand and dragged her after him.

"When did you get this?"

"After I sold the Jag."

Her brows shot up. "You sold it?"

"Didn't I just say that?"

She jerked free. "I'm not going anywhere with you when you're mad."

He sighed and came to her. In an instant he gathered her in his arms and kissed her senseless. "Come with me, please."

"Since you asked nicely." Not that she ever

thought of resisting, she thought, climbing into the ATV and examining the interior. There was an infant-care seat in the rear, and her heart turned to mush. She faced front as he got in and started the engine. He didn't talk, driving onto the highway, listening to country music.

"Where are we going?"

He wiggled his brows, ever silent, and her pulse accelerated with anticipation. He pulled in front of a large white house with dark green shutters. Madison climbed out of the truck. It was beautiful. Lowcountry style with a wrap-around porch and a waist-high fence around the yard. There wasn't another house within four acres.

"Whose is it?"

Taking her hand, he strode up the porch and opened the door before stepping back. "Ours."

She blinked. "What?"

He gave her a push inside.

Madison liked the outside and fell in love with the inside. Spacious with plenty of windows. A formal living room and dining room, but as she stepped into the kitchen, she couldn't help but smile. It was huge, the counter overlooking a Carolina room, a dining slash family-room area with a river stone fireplace and a bank of windows and French doors.

Alex leaned against the frame, watching her run her hand over the counter, poke in cabinets. The look on her face told him more than she said, and he nearly groaned with relief. Now for the big guns.

"Come on." He turned out of the kitchen and walked through the foyer to the hall. There were four bedrooms and an office. He stopped in front of the room across from the master suite and pushed open the door.

Madison stepped inside and lost her breath.

It was the only room with furniture. Baby furniture. The decorating was detailed down to the pattern on the rug and the trim on the curtains. The nursery was filled: a high chair, cradle and crib, a stroller, stuffed toys, clothes. There was nothing more that a child needed. Their child.

She spun around and found him close.

Pushing up against her body, he gripped her arms, gazing deeply into her eyes. "I love you, Maddy."

Her heart jumped every time he said it. "Why did you do all this?"

"I couldn't think of any other way to convince you that I'm ready for commitment. For sixty years or so." He gathered her close, gazing into her eyes. "I've been going through the motions of living, and I felt as if I didn't belong to anything or anyone. I lost my way. Till you found me. You showed me everything I was missing and let me touch all I could have. I know you are capable of taking care of our child alone, but you don't have to. I won't let you. It's time for you, time for us. We'll do this *together*. I love you."

She swallowed repeatedly. "I'm afraid that love isn't enough."

The question in her voice slayed him. "Does anyone know if it's enough? Does any one person know exactly how to make a marriage work, or how to raise a child? We all take the risk. I'm terrified of losing this one chance, and all I am certain of right now is that I want to spend my life loving you."

Her eyes watered. Oh, how she loved this man.

"This is our house. Where we start our life. Our new beginning. And see?" He brushed back the curtain. A good hundred yards away, near the edge of the woods, lay a cottage similar to the house. There was a plowed garden plot beside it.

"Your dad can come live here, and you can fuss over him all you want."

"But Claire—"

"Claire has her college paid for, a nanny for her son and a place of her own, just as she wanted."

"Alex, I can't ask you to—"

He silenced her with a strong kiss. "You didn't ask. That's what's so incredible about you, baby, you never ask for yourself. Now I'm asking for *us*. I've spent my whole life missing the good things, simple joys, and the reason why people fall in love and have kids and stay married for fifty years. I've missed your laughter, your jokes. I can't survive without you, darlin', so I'm begging. Marry me. Put me out of my misery with your twelve-gauge or just say 'I do.' I'm not ready to be your man...I *am* your man." His eyes grew suspiciously glossy. "Now I want to be your husband." He covered her still-flat tummy. "And a daddy."

"Alexander," she said in a slow drawl that left him shaking. "I do love you so."

The corners of his eyes crinkled with his smile, and between thumb and forefinger he held up a ring, a proper diamond solitaire. "Believe in me, baby. You're the only one who matters."

A tear rolled down her cheek. "Yes, I'll marry you." He slipped it on her finger, his relief palpable as he closed his arms tightly around her, burying his face in the curve of her throat. He trembled in her arms, and Madison smoothed her hands over his broad back.

"Thank God you said yes," he muttered, then rained kisses over her face. "The decorator comes on Monday."

She pulled back and met his gaze, sniffling. "You were so sure of yourself?"

With his thumb he swiped tears from her cheeks. "With you, I'm never sure of a damn thing. But I was going to camp out on your doorstep until *you* committed to *me*."

She smiled, a smile that lifted his heart, and Alex crushed her in his arms and knew he'd found a home. A real home. And a place to belong, not in the structure surrounding him, but in the woman in his arms.

# Epilogue

"We haven't decided on a name."

"Now is *not* the time, Alexander." Madison nodded to the obstetrician and rose up, pushing, panting, pushing, the obstetrician like a quarterback ready for the catch. Alexander, bless him, mopped her brow, held her upright and labored with her as she forced their child out. The poor man was going to rupture something vital.

"That's it, Mrs. Donahue, keep going, keep going," the doctor urged.

"*I am.*"

"Almost."

"Only wins in horseshoes," she muttered, took a deep breath and pushed. She strained for what seemed like minutes, then let out a rebel yell of triumph and freedom, and sank onto the labor bed.

"You did it, baby."

''Not like I had a choice, huh?'' she gasped.

''It's a boy!'' the doctor said and Alex choked as his son's wail filled the delivery room. After measurements and tests, they placed the child in his arms and tended to Madison. Her eyes never left her husband as he held their child reverently and dropped a tender kiss to his forehead. Then Alex came to her, laying their son in her arms.

''He's beautiful. I never thought anyone fell in love at first sight,'' Alex whispered, unmindful of the tears streaking his lean cheeks.

''Gee, I thought that's what happened with you and me?''

He looked at her then, smiling. ''Yeah, it was. Those legs got me.'' He crawled into the bed with her, snuggling his new family close as the nurses and doctor left the room. ''Thank you, baby.'' From his pocket he withdrew a gold bracelet and clasped it over her wrist.

She stared at her son's birthstones encrusted in the gold. ''Oh, *Alexander*.''

He still loved the way she said his name, slow and sultry.

''I never forgot what you looked like holding Shannon, never forgot how much at that moment, I wished it was my baby you held.''

She was astonished. ''You never said.''

''I was too scared to even dream then, Maddy.''

''And now?''

''You *are* my dreams.''

He could spend his life looking at her, and his throat tightened when he realized again just how lucky he was to be in love with this woman and to have her love him back. She'd awakened him, made him feel alive and hungry for life. Her very presence reminded him that love came to them in so many small, simple ways, and how easy it was to give, if he would just let it happen.

Alexander pressed a kiss to her soft, brown curls and silently thanked God that he'd bid on a wife for hire...and had come home with the real thing.

*    *    *    *    *

*Be sure to watch for the next romance in the* THE BRIDAL BID *promotion,*

*THE COWBOY TAKES A BRIDE*

*by Cathleen Galitz, coming next month only to Silhouette Desire.*

## SILHOUETTE® *Desire®*

### AND

# Peggy Moreland

Bring you another warm, wonderful and
downright sexy book in Peggy's miniseries

### TEXAS BRIDES

Come on down to the McCloud family ranch—'cause
there's no place like Texas for a wedding!

### *On sale in January 2000:*

### HARD LOVIN' MAN
### Silhouette Desire #1270

Long-lost half sister Lacey Cline, the newest member
of the McCloud family, will be the next bride to walk
down the aisle at the McCloud ranch—if she can
rope and tie Travis Cordell, the most ornery,
most irresistible bachelor in Texas!

*The fun continues this spring, with
Peggy Moreland's new miniseries,*

# TEXAS GROOMS

You won't want to miss these rugged rodeo men and
the women they love! Only from Peggy Moreland
and Silhouette Desire.

*Available at your favorite retail outlet.*

Visit us at www.romance.net

SDTB

If you enjoyed what you just read,
then we've got an offer you can't resist!

# Take 2 bestselling love stories FREE!

# Plus get a FREE surprise gift!

---

**Clip this page and mail it to Silhouette Reader Service™**

| **IN U.S.A.** | **IN CANADA** |
|---|---|
| 3010 Walden Ave. | P.O. Box 609 |
| P.O. Box 1867 | Fort Erie, Ontario |
| Buffalo, N.Y. 14240-1867 | L2A 5X3 |

**YES!** Please send me 2 free Silhouette Desire® novels and my free surprise gift. Then send me 6 brand-new novels every month, which I will receive months before they're available in stores. In the U.S.A., bill me at the bargain price of $3.12 plus 25¢ delivery per book and applicable sales tax, if any*. In Canada, bill me at the bargain price of $3.49 plus 25¢ delivery per book and applicable taxes**. That's the complete price and a savings of over 10% off the cover prices—what a great deal! I understand that accepting the 2 free books and gift places me under no obligation ever to buy any books. I can always return a shipment and cancel at any time. Even if I never buy another book from Silhouette, the 2 free books and gift are mine to keep forever. So why not take us up on our invitation. You'll be glad you did!

225 SEN CNFA
326 SEN CNFC

| Name | (PLEASE PRINT) | |
|---|---|---|
| Address | Apt.# | |
| City | State/Prov. | Zip/Postal Code |

\* Terms and prices subject to change without notice. Sales tax applicable in N.Y.
\*\* Canadian residents will be charged applicable provincial taxes and GST.
  All orders subject to approval. Offer limited to one per household.
  ® are registered trademarks of Harlequin Enterprises Limited.

DES99                                    ©1998 Harlequin Enterprises Limited

**Start celebrating Silhouette's 20th anniversary
with these 4 special titles by
*New York Times* bestselling authors**

*Fire and Rain**
**by Elizabeth Lowell**

*King of the Castle*
**by Heather Graham Pozzessere**

*State Secrets**
**by Linda Lael Miller**

*Paint Me Rainbows**
**by Fern Michaels**

On sale in December 1999

**Plus, a special free book offer inside each title!**

*Available at your favorite retail outlet*
*\*Also available on audio from Brilliance.*

_Silhouette_®
*Where love comes alive™*

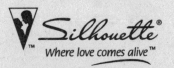